Jack slowly en
within his, gen
atop her skin
hand was enveloped in his.
"You're shaking. Are you cold?"

Dixie knew she could lie, but what was the point? "No, I'm not cold."

At his soft intake of breath, Dixie thrust her chin forward. Scared or not, she'd pretend a boldness she was far from feeling. Hadn't she decided she was tired of life passing her by?

Jack reached forward and traced a finger down her cheek. "If you're not cold, why are you shaking?"

This was it, the moment of truth. It was time to make one of those pivotal decisions in her life.

Dixie took a deep breath. "I'm afraid."

Jack frowned, evidently surprised by her answer. "Of me?"

Dixie took half a step closer. "No—afraid I don't have the nerve to kiss you. And more afraid you won't want me to."

Jodi Dawson spent years dreaming about happily-ever-after before realising she could make it happen in life, as well as in her books. Having lived in over ten of the United States, and for a year in South Korea, she has a passion for travel and adventure. She has been a teacher, retail manager, amusement park employee, and goat milker, but now follows her heart and writes romantic fiction. Her most sincere desire is to bring a smile to the reader's face and have her finish her books feeling refreshed and believing in every possibility. You can look Jodi up on-line at: www.jodidawson.com

Recent titles by the same author:

ASSIGNMENT: MARRIAGE
THEIR MIRACLE BABY
HER SECRET MILLIONAIRE

FIRST PRIZE: MARRIAGE

BY
JODI DAWSON

MILLS & BOON and MILLS & BOON with the Rose Device are registered trademarks of the publisher.

First published in Great Britain 2005
Harlequin Mills & Boon Limited,
Eton House, 18-24 Paradise Road, Richmond, Surrey TW9 1SR

© Jodi Beyes 2005

ISBN 0 263 84221 5

Set in Times Roman 10½ on 12½ pt.
02-0305-41546

Printed and bound in Spain
by Litografía Rosés, S.A., Barcelona

CHAPTER ONE

…hopes and dreams and the possibility of it all…

"HOLD on to your hems, ladies. It's a skirt alert day, with wind gusts up to sixty miles per hour along the Front Range."

Dixie Osborn grimaced at the smooth-voiced disc jockey's attempt at humor. She wasn't in the mood. Glaring through her cracked windshield at the rush hour traffic clogging the roadway, she wondered for the thousandth time why she was knocking herself out trying to get downtown.

The voice from the radio reminded her of the reason. "Only twenty minutes remaining before one lucky listener wins our 'Chance of a Lifetime' drawing. Remember, you *must* be present to win."

Thankfully, a jazz saxophone replaced the overly cheerful voice drifting from her car speaker, the one still functioning.

Dixie glanced at the temperature gauge on the dash and prayed for the indicator to remain between the R and M of "normal." If it crept higher, she'd never make it. She glared at the minivan spewing exhaust in front of her. The gasping chug of her near-dead compact contrasted with the rumble of the sports car to the left. So much for the shortcut—it seemed half the population of Denver knew about it.

Drumming her chewed nails on the steering wheel, she contemplated the possible legal penalty for abandoning her heap and schlepping the remainder of the way. It would certainly be faster.

Static crackled through the radio speaker as Dixie frantically fiddled with the dial until the annoying voice returned. "The crowd is growing restless here outside the Miner's Lady Grill at the Sixteenth Street Mall. Brick Dingle here, your afternoon deejay, bringing you our 'Chance of a Lifetime' contest."

Puhleeze, what kind of name is Brick Dingle?

Nosing over, she waved at the trucker who'd taken pity on her and eased over into his lane.

"Only ten minutes until someone walks away with the grand prize. One of the two hundred people entered will receive the title to the Crazy Creek Lodge nestled in the beautiful high country of the Rocky Mountains—"

Applause and whistles drowned the rest of the speech.

I'll never make it.

Turning up a one-way street only two blocks from where she wanted to be, Dixie caught sight of the chance she needed. An empty delivery spot in front of a high-rise building sat vacant. For once, not considering the consequences of parking illegally, she squeezed into the miniscule space and killed the engine.

Grabbing her backpack, she wiggled through the

driver's side window. She really needed to see about getting the door fixed.

Sprinting across the street, she ignored the blaring horns from irate drivers. Her watch showed only four minutes left until the drawing. Praying silently, she deftly dodged pedestrians and ignored the stitch in her side.

Thank God she'd worn jeans. Friday was casual day at the Center, so the running shoes and denim worked to her advantage.

The crowd ahead showed where she needed to be, but that didn't mean she was there. Ignoring the odd looks and sharp elbows, she managed to maneuver near the radio booth.

"Hey, you here for the drawing?" A grunge-dressed teen with dreadlocks grinned at her.

"Yeah." She avoided eye contact. *If he hits on me, I'll die.*

At twenty-seven, she knew she looked a decade younger. It was her own fault, as her mother liked to remind her. So what? Dixie didn't care for makeup and liked her long hair bound in a braid. Her lack of glamour didn't bother her students and it certainly didn't bother her.

Just keep telling yourself that, Osborn.

A chill raced across her skin as the April breeze teased her, reminding her that winter might have passed on the calendar, but in Colorado, spring was a day-to-day thing with no guarantees. Zipping the fleece jacket to her neck, Dixie shoved her hands into her pockets. Where the devil were her gloves?

Probably in the pile of muck in her back seat with everything else she couldn't find.

"It's time, folks. KOSE brings you the 'Chance of a Lifetime' drawing."

Dixie stood on tiptoe and tried to catch a glimpse of the man offering the future she needed.

"Wanna sit on my shoulders?"

She glared at the teen. Surely she'd misunderstood him. "Excuse me?"

He backed up a step and held his hands up. "Just thought you'd be able to see better."

Dixie shook her head. It wasn't the kid's fault she was a bundle of raw nerves. "Thanks, but I can see fine." Turning back toward the deejay's booth, she slipped between two businessmen and found herself at the front of the crowd.

"Mr. Granger, from the independent accounting firm of Granger, Flitch and Becker, will pull the winning entry from our barrel."

Dixie caught her first glimpse of the man behind the voice and nearly giggled. The man with the smooth chocolate tone was at least three inches shorter than her five feet and at least thirty years older. Not quite the virile specimen she'd imagined while listening to him on the radio.

Ah, well, fantasies were never quite the same as real life.

The murmur of voices stilled, as the crowd seemed to collectively hold its breath. Dixie's heart pounded as Mr. Granger reached to turn the handle on the barrel. Three times it turned as white slips of paper tumbled over and around each other within the meshed steel cage.

Please, please, please. She knew her chances were slim, but she wanted it so badly and the kids at the center needed it. Didn't that count for something?

"Now, Mr. Granger, if you'll draw the winning entry, I'm sure the crowd wants to be put out of its misery."

Granger gave a semblance of a smile and plunged his hand into the mass of entries.

Dixie tensed and concentrated on every move, as if she could will his fingers to close on the paper with her name scrawled on it. Her breath slipped between parted lips in quick gasps and she gripped the straps of her backpack with icy fingers.

The accountant withdrew his hand with a scrap of white clenched inside his fist. The crowd surged forward and Dixie found herself shuffled and almost knocked off balance.

"Here it is, the moment you've waited for." The disc jockey held his hand out to accept the paper. "Are you ready, Denver?"

Cheers and screams rose from the crowd as Dixie tried to hear what the man was saying.

"...the winner of the Crazy Creek Lodge is—uh-oh." Pulling the microphone away from his mouth, the deejay consulted with Granger and several men in suits standing nearby.

What's wrong? Dixie sensed the question passing through the crowd as it silently screamed inside her head.

Brick Dingle nodded at the circle of suits surrounding him and lifted the microphone. "Ladies and gentlemen, things just got interesting."

Murmurs ran though the crowd.

"Seems one of our contestants likes sweets. A smear of chocolate has *glued* two of the entries together."

It couldn't be.

Dixie had licked most of the stuff off her fingers before she'd shoved her entry into the box. Why couldn't she stick to granola bars? But, realistically, what were the odds it was *her* chocolate?

"After we announce the winners, if our two finalists will step forward and show identification we'll find out just how interesting things can get." Dingle cleared his throat as his fingers separated the papers. "The first name is…are you ready, folks?"

For Heaven's sake, just say it already so I can get on with my life. The not knowing was torture—it would be better once someone else won. Then she would stop hoping for the impossible.

"Ms. Dixie Osborn, will you come forward?" Dingle shouted.

Numbness spread through Dixie's body and her vision narrowed to focus on the paper in Brick Dingle's hand. She'd heard wrong—wanted to hear her name so badly that her imagination had conjured it.

"Ms. Osborn, you have two minutes before your name is withdrawn. Now let's find out who was stuck to the lady…"

Dixie forced her legs to propel her body forward. As she brushed past people and stepped in front of the crowd, they turned and started cheering. Heat crept into her face as she realized how many people were watching her.

"...come on up."

Amidst the noise and confusion, she'd missed the second name, but it didn't matter. Stopping in front of the table, she cleared her throat. "I'm...I'm Dixie Osborn," she squeaked.

"Folks, this little lady here is talking, and I can't hear her." Dingle quieted the crowd and pushed a microphone in front of her mouth. "What did you say, honey?"

Suddenly the center of attention, Dixie forced herself to ignore the press of people behind her. "I'm Dixie Osborn."

"Ah, and here comes our second finalist."

She turned to watch the throng separate as someone passed toward the front. Breaking through the last of the crowd, her competition stepped into view.

Oh, my stars. Only nervous tension kept Dixie's jaw from dropping as a bear of a man approached.

Confident strides carried the giant toward her. As he advanced, she could see that although he was tall, it was his broad shoulders that contributed to the sense of size. Hair black as a moonless night framed a face that might have been carved from the mountains on the horizon.

As he flashed his driver's license, Dixie remembered hers, and showed it to the deejay.

Stopping in front of her, the other finalist's piercing blue gaze pinned her to the spot. "So, you like chocolate."

Dixie nodded, unable to form a coherent sentence. *It's just a man. Pull yourself together before he makes off with your lodge.*

Dingle stepped around the table. "You must be Jack Powers."

The man turned and shook hands with the deejay. "Yes, sir. Now, what happens?"

"Since our entries were stuck together, how do you choose?" Dixie grimaced at the sound of her voice—it emerged breathless and husky, rather than confident and strong.

"I'm a firm believer in ladies first." A small smile pulled at her adversary's lips. "I'm sure you understand that right now neither of us has won anything."

Who the hell did he think he was? No way would she bow out gracefully while he made off with the future of the center.

"Look here, Mr.—"

"Now, now." The deejay glanced back and forth between them. "Although the station never expected anything like this to happen, our independent accounting firm has planned for any contingency."

Dixie turned from the man standing too close and concentrated on the accountant who held an envelope in his hand.

"Mr. Granger, if you'll open and read the plan for a tie, I'm sure our lucky contestants are eager to hear what you have to say."

Lucky was the last thing Dixie felt. How had her dream turned into a nightmare when she was so close to everything she needed? Glancing sideways, she was struck again by the sheer muscle of the man waiting for the same answer she wanted. The pull of the black T-shirt across his chest caused her mind to skitter like a drunken crab. She reluctantly forced her gaze back to the accountant.

Focus, Dixie, focus.

Mr. Granger carefully opened the envelope and stared at the sheet of paper he removed. "In the event of a tie, it is determined that the parties involved will reside jointly at the lodge for four days and three nights. If both parties are still present on the final day, the deed of ownership will be decided by a coin toss."

Laughs and jeers sounded from the mass of humanity around them. Great. She had to spend several days alone with the Neanderthal man with an entitlement problem that made him think everything was his. It just kept getting worse and worse, but she wasn't giving up. Peeking upward and sideways, she saw a frown pull at the corner of Jack Powers' lips.

Brick Dingle laughed. "Sounds like an intriguing twist. What do our two finalists have to say?"

Dixie's thoughts bounded and bumped over each other. Mentally she started the list of things she'd have to do—take leave from her job, arrange care for her dog, and a million other chores, but at this moment none of them mattered. Meeting her rival's stare without flinching, she offered her hand. "I accept the challenge. Good luck, Mr. Powers."

He put sunglasses on and accepted her hand, engulfed it in his. "The same to you, Ms. Osborn." His sunglasses couldn't conceal the stubbornness of his jawline.

Warmth seeped into her fingers at his firm grip. Dixie didn't have a choice but to win, the kids were counting on her. A cheer went up around them as she released his hand.

"Stay tuned to KOSE to find out how this turns out, listeners. We'll keep you posted," Dingle promised. "It should prove very entertaining."

Dixie grinned like an idiot as the biggest obstacle to her goal stood next to her. Interesting or hellish, it didn't matter. She was going to win the Crazy Creek Lodge if it killed her.

What am I going to tell Emma? What has she gotten me mixed up in?

Although he'd been less than thrilled when his aunt Emma told him she'd entered his name in the radio contest, Jack knew how much the dream of the lodge in the mountains meant to her. But he felt a bit of guilt, too. Jack was tied to win the lodge with someone who'd entered the contest...*he* was a proxy for Emma.

And her dreams.

Jack crossed his arms over his chest and tried to look intimidating. Although from his angle, it didn't appear effective. Rather than looking suitably impressed by his glower and backing down, Dixie Osborn glared back at him and jutted her chin forward.

And her chest. *Hmm.* She didn't seem to realize her determined posture angled her rounded breasts impudently at him, also. Maybe three nights with the perky miss wouldn't be so bad.

No way—a woman was the last thing he needed right now. Winning the lodge was too important to Emma to allow himself to be distracted by thoughts of rolling around on a bearskin rug with Miss Dixie Osborn.

Jack glanced at Dixie again, wondering if she'd try to use her charms to persuade him to let her have the prize, but he could handle it. Emma depended on him—he wouldn't forget her. Or let her down. His entire focus would be on taking care of her. On trying to win the contest for her.

I will resist temptation. Glancing again at Dixie Osborn's chest, he nearly groaned aloud. Good try—he'd just have to ignore the woman.

Spinning away from him, Dixie faced the accountant. "So all we have to do is stay at the lodge for four days, right?"

Jack stared at the view of snug denim covering a toned bottom she unwittingly offered him. Shaking his head, he glanced at the crowd milling around them. He'd been undercover too long—he needed to get out and have some fun.

"The condition of the lodge is 'questionable.'" Mr. Granger's voice squeaked on the last word.

The accountant's words drew Jack's attention. "How questionable?"

Running a finger under his collar, the man cleared his throat. "Well, the former owner closed the lodge to guests over twenty years ago and never let anyone in or near the place."

Jack didn't like it. "Why doesn't the radio station know its condition? Is it habitable?"

"The condition was never mentioned in the contest advertising."

"Will there be electricity or water?" Dixie tapped her foot. "Just what *do* you know about the place?"

Well, she's no wimp. Maybe it would be tougher to convince her to give up the lodge than he'd thought.

Rather than answering, Mr. Granger pulled two sheets of paper from the envelope. "This is a map to the lodge. You will begin your stay in two days, at exactly 10:00 a.m. If you'll sign these waivers releasing the radio station and our accounting firm from all responsibility concerning the lodge's condition, we'll be done for now."

"How will you know whether we show up or not?" Jack glanced at the map he held and noted that Dixie nibbled her lower lip as she read hers. So the lady was nervous. Perhaps it would only take a coyote's howl to send her packing.

"You'll police each other better than anyone, since the lodge is at stake." The accountant stuck his hand out, then seemed to reconsider when Jack cocked an eyebrow. "Well, at any rate, good luck. I will arrive at noon on the fourth day to verify both of you are still present and to execute the coin toss, if necessary.''

As the man turned to leave, Dixie reached out and grabbed his jacket sleeve. ''Uh, will there be a chaperone or something?'' A splash of pink tinged her cheeks.

She's uncomfortable about being alone with me? Maybe Jack could leer in her direction and keep her from showing up. Naw, he couldn't do it. Intimidating a woman wasn't his style. Besides, she'd probably take one look at the primitive surroundings and hightail it home anyway, if she could even locate the place.

He decided to soothe her ruffled feathers. ''Miss Osborn, I assure you I'm safe.''

Her eyebrows shot upward. ''Mr. Powers, no offense, but I'm sure most criminals don't advertise their intentions.''

''If you'd like to forfeit now…'' He waited for her to quit, but hoped she wouldn't. A bit of friendly competition might prove interesting. And he still felt a twinge of guilt over not even entering himself.

After staring at him with her green-eyed gaze for several seconds, she shook her head. ''No, I won't give up that easily. Too much is at stake.''

Like what? Just why did the fresh-faced woman want a lodge in the wilderness? Was she some kind of tree hugging, hippie wannabe?

Nodding, he grinned at her. ''Then I guess I'll see you in two days.''

She flipped the thick, black braid over her shoulder. ''Count on it. And four days after that, you can kiss the Crazy Creek Lodge goodbye.''

CHAPTER TWO

Two hours later, Jack slipped a manila folder across the top of his desk toward his client. He ignored the smell of stale cigarettes and fried food oozing from the direction of the man across from him. Probably a thousand-dollar Italian suit on the guy and the man still looked like a sleazeball.

The phrase "can't judge a book by its cover" took on a whole new meaning.

Jack cleared his throat. "As you can see by the photographs, your suspicions about your wife's relationship with her personal trainer were verified."

Glancing toward the images of the passionate embraces of the couple caught on film, Jack frowned. After several meetings with the "wronged" hubby, Jack had begun to understand the woman's need to find attention elsewhere. But it wasn't his job to judge, only to capture evidence on film. He hated to, but maybe he'd go back to investigating industrial espionage. At least he could separate his personal feelings from the black and white world of corporate America.

"These are great." Mr. Boyd cackled, not appearing upset by the concrete evidence of his wife's infidelity. "Now the witch can't screw me in court over the thing with my secretary."

Great—such a noble reason to be a private detective. Why hadn't Jack listened to his uncle Vincent and taken over the family dry cleaning business?

Yeah, sure. "About final payment…"

The man reached a fleshy hand inside his jacket and pulled out a wad of cash. He peeled several bills from the stack and tossed the money on the desk. "That'll cover it. Nice doin' business with ya."

Long after Boyd vacated the groaning chair, Jack stared at the money. The overwhelming need to douse it with disinfectant still pulsed through him. When had the job lost its glamour? He liked being his own boss and calling the shots, didn't he?

Of course he did—he was just burnt out on too many cheating spouse cases. Wasn't anyone faithful anymore?

A timid knock sounded on the frosted glass of his door.

"Come on in, Emma, he's gone." No one else had the same hunch-shouldered, timid stance as his great-aunt and secretary.

"That man gives me the creeps." Tucking a strand of gray hair into her topknot, she shuddered. "Makes me wonder why I left my job at the coroner's office."

"Because you love me and can't stand dead bodies." He spun his chair and stared through the window at the brick wall across the alley. "Did you manage to postpone the investigation at Reynolds?"

Heels clicking on the floor, she stepped into his line of vision. "Of course, but are you sure about this? I know you weren't exactly thrilled with my having entered you in the contest."

No, he wasn't sure of anything, but he had to try. "Am I ready to overlook you putting my name in the hat for some radio contest? It's done. Am I sure I want to leave the rewarding world of investigating to run a lodge? Oh, I think I'll get used to the idea. You're not backing out on your offer to do the book-keeping *if* we win the lodge, are you?"

A glow shimmered in her eyes, evidence of her excitement at the prospect. "Oh, no. You know I'll help out wherever you need me. I hoped you'd win, but never really thought they'd pull your name. You work too hard, I thought this would be good for you. I just want you to be happy."

Yes, he knew that. Emma had practically raised him and loved him as her own after his parents died. She'd sacrificed and scrimped to ensure he went to college, always putting him first. Now, it was his turn to put Emma first. She deserved more than a second floor tenement in her golden years. With the lodge Emma had set her heart on, he'd make sure she relaxed and enjoyed life.

"Well, things aren't solid yet." Jack admitted. "I still have to make it through four days in the sticks and a coin toss." He rubbed his forehead. "I'm betting Ms. Osborn will cut and run halfway through the first night. Wild animals, strange noises, and all."

Emma chuckled. "What makes you think she can't take it?"

Remembering the determination in the little spitfire's gaze, he tapped a finger against his knee. Dixie was a fighter—he liked fighters. "You might be right. She seemed scrappy, as well as cute."

"Cute?" Emma sounded interested.

"In a gangly, puppy kind of way. Don't get any matchmaking ideas. This is pure competition—nothing personal." Ignoring the protest coming from the testosterone center of his brain, he continued. "Besides, she looked about nineteen. Maybe her parents won't let her run off to the mountains with a stranger."

Emma walked toward the door. "Just the same, I won't tender my resignation until the four days are over."

"Start typing it—that lodge is as good as yours." He hoped. He had to win for Emma's sake, nothing would distract Jack from his goal. Not even a green-eyed temptress in body-hugging denim.

Dixie paused in her packing to scratch the top of Sadie's head. The golden retriever didn't realize Dixie was on a deadline and had to finish within a few hours. Scanning the various piles scattered about the living room, Dixie blew a strand of hair from her face. It looked as though a small storm had whipped through her apartment. Hmm, maybe she could petition the governor into declaring it a national disaster area.

"Well, girl, what the heck should I take?" The dog nudged under her arm. "Besides you—I already said you could come." A few days of fresh air and exercise would be good for both of them, plus Sadie would make her feel safer. Although all Powers would have to do was look cross-eyed and the dog would wet herself and pass out. Oh well, Sadie was better than nothing.

As Dixie reached for her hiking boots, the ringing doorbell demanded her attention. "Come on in, Maggie. It's open."

She watched as her friend peered around the edge of the door with a look of exaggerated horror, before stepping carefully over a sleeping bag. "Oh, knock it off, Maggie, it's not that bad, is it?"

"Hon, I've been gone for over an hour and it looks worse than when I left. What in the world are you trying to do?" Maggie yanked her oversize purse higher on her shoulder, balanced a pizza box in one hand and waved toward the kitchen. "You grab plates and I'll pack for you."

"You're a prize." Dixie stood and grinned. "Just make sure it's what I'll need for a few days in the woods." She took the pizza and stepped into the kitchen.

"So, they couldn't give you any information about utilities?" Maggie's voice carried easily in the small space. "Are you sure about this? I mean, you don't even know the guy."

Loaded down with napkins and paper plates, Dixie wandered back into the living room. "No, and he's not likely to try anything since the radio station knows who he is. He'd be the first suspect if I end up buried out back."

"You know what I mean. What if he tries to seduce you or something?"

"Not likely—I don't normally drive men into fits of passion. Besides, you didn't see him. The man is gorgeous—he probably has a buxom blonde waiting at home." Dixie peeled a slice of pizza from the box. "The last thing I have time for is a man."

Maggie stared at her as if she'd uttered a blasphemous statement. "There's *always* time for a man."

Resisting the urge to giggle at her friend's outraged expression, Dixie bit into the droopy pizza. She'd tried too many times to convince Maggie she wasn't interested in a relationship, that her job and dog were fulfilling enough. Most of the time Dixie even managed to convince herself. Only the occasional nighttime fantasy made her long for more, but dreams aside, she had a goal. A man wasn't part of it.

"Any word on the bank's extension?"

Maggie's words pulled Dixie back to reality and the reason she needed the lodge. "No, and the teen crisis center needs a permanent location—our funding is almost depleted. I'm hoping if I can turn a profit with this lodge, we can convince the bank to extend a mortgage option for the center using the lodge as collateral."

Wiping her mouth with a napkin, Maggie shook her head. "Just don't get your hopes up, honey, it's a long shot."

"Right now it's our *only* shot. We need that lodge."

Sadie snatched a pepperoni that landed at Dixie's feet. Wagging her tail proudly, Sadie begged for more.

"I don't think so—learn some manners." Tossing a piece of crust onto her plate, Dixie sent her most forlorn and pitiful look in Maggie's direction. "Are you sure you wouldn't like to come with me? It would be a mini-vacation."

"Not on your life, girlfriend. Living in the sticks might be your dream, but I get hives just thinking about all that stuff." She poked another bite into her mouth.

"What 'stuff'?"

"You know—trees, animals…things." Her words were muffled as they squeezed past the pizza.

"Excuses—we have those things right here in the city."

"Yeah, but they're caged or houseplants. Don't worry, I'll visit if you win the place." Maggie shooed her away. "Now, make the kitchen sanitary while I try to pack."

What a friend, offering to pack. Scrubbing the baked-on mess off the stovetop, Dixie mentally ran through her list again. Arrange leave from work. No problem. Bring Sadie's toys and food. Check. Let her neighbor Mrs. Underwood know Dixie would be away from her apartment for a few days—no sense worrying her landlady. Dixie had stopped by earlier to tell her. Done. Call Mother.

Dixie smacked her forehead with a sudsy hand. *I knew I forgot something.* A little subconscious slip-up—God forbid her mother should find out about Jack Powers and the lodge. Dixie knew she had to call before she left. If Dixie didn't call and her mother phoned and heard the answering machine repeatedly, she'd have the National Guard looking for her only child before the state knew what hit it. Dixie would at least leave a message.

"Make sure you leave the location of the lodge," Maggie yelled from the bedroom.

"I wrote it on the pad by the phone. It's just outside of Pagosa Springs." *Only eighteen miles from civilization.* "Are you almost done?" She wandered into the living room.

Maggie stepped out of the bedroom. "Just finished."

Dixie glanced around the room. Where disorganization once reigned, order was restored. "How do you do it?"

"What?"

"Take five minutes to complete a task I couldn't finish in a day?" She plopped onto the sofa.

"Your skills are with people, mine are with things. That's why you make a great counselor and I make a marvelous fashion buyer." Maggie sat with both legs curled beneath her. "Now, tell me again about this Powers fellow."

Why couldn't Maggie focus on the lodge rather than the nuisance of a man? Groaning, Dixie closed her eyes and recounted the tale for the tenth time that evening.

"My entry had chocolate on it..."

*   *   *

Jack cursed as another mammoth pothole jarred his truck sideways. Tigger yelped and scrambled for footing on the seat next to him. Downshifting, Jack eased up on the accelerator while he scanned the pockmarked roadway for the best path. Jack reached over and gave the large, shaking mutt a reassuring pat and was rewarded with a wet tongue against the side of his face.

Another hole shook the truck's frame and rattled Jack's teeth. Had the military used this area to test land mines? Judging by the condition of the roads he'd been on for the last hour of the six-hour drive, it seemed a definite possibility. If he won the lodge for Emma, the road was the first thing he'd fix.

Swinging the wheel wide, he maneuvered around a hairpin turn. How much farther? The man at the ranger station had pinpointed the spot on the map. Now all Jack had to do was find it. Simple—huh— nice of the radio station to omit distance from the map.

At least he knew if it were this rough on his pickup, Dixie Osborn probably wouldn't find the place at all.

Breaking out of the thick ponderosa pines, he caught sight of a log structure on the edge of a meadow, next to an orange, late-model car.

There was no way she'd beaten him here, but who else would be in the middle of nowhere in a vehicle totally unsuited for the terrain?

As though confirming his suspicions, Dixie

bounced around the corner of the building, her arms filled with pinecones.

Great, she's a Mother Nature type. Or worse, a clone of that television decorating lady Emma liked to watch.

Pulling next to her excuse for a car, he killed the engine and opened his door. Catching sight of him, Dixie stopped abruptly and spilled her cargo.

She turned back toward the trees and whistled.

What the devil? He grabbed Tigger's collar to keep the dog from bounding out of the truck.

Dixie dropped onto her heels and held her arms open. "Come on, girl."

A golden retriever greeted her with a long tongue and wiggling body. Tigger strained to pull free and join in the lovefest. Great—his big, orange-colored mutt was turning sissy on him after only one glimpse of the woman and her fancy dog. It was going to be a long four days.

Laughing, Dixie stood and faced him. Her unbound hair flowed about her face, brushing her waist. The sight brought visions of the length draped across his bare chest. His body tightened.

Dang, why couldn't she be an eighty-year-old grandmother?

Clipping a leash to Tigger's collar, Jack approached temptation an inch at a time. "How the heck did you beat me up here? It's a six-hour drive from Denver."

"I drove up last night and stayed in Pagosa Springs. I wanted to see the lodge at sunrise." She blushed at the admission and looked at Tigger. "You have a beautiful dog."

Tigger eased to where she held her dog by the collar. Cautiously the dogs sniffed each other before wagging their tails like long-lost relations.

"Looks like they'll get along." Jack watched the healthy color fade from Dixie's face as he released Tigger from the leash. "What's wrong?"

"He's a boy." Dismay filled her words.

"You mean Tigger?"

One side of her mouth tipped upward. "You named your dog Tigger?"

"My great-aunt named him."

"Oh…Sadie's female."

"Okay." Was he missing the point?

"A female in heat."

"So—oh." The interest Tigger showed Sadie took on a new meaning. "That could be interesting."

"She's scheduled to go to a breeder when I get back." Color crept up her neck. "To be…well…you know."

Was she embarrassed to discuss her dog's sex life? Evidently so. "I'll watch Tigger, but it'll be tough. Sadie seems to like him."

The two dogs wrestled and chased each other before they collapsed side by side beneath the shade of an aspen tree.

While Dixie watched the dogs and nibbled her lower lip, Jack watched Dixie. Even in a faded sweatshirt and jeans, her form was enticing. The naked skin of her face and dark hair brushing her cheek reminded him he'd told Emma that Dixie looked nineteen. "How old are you?"

Startled, she stared at him for several seconds before answering. "Twenty-seven, why?"

"Has anyone ever told you that—"

"I look like a teenager? Yes, constantly. Have *you* ever been carded trying to buy lottery tickets?" She grinned at him. "Luckily, in my line of work, it helps to look young."

"You work undercover for the cops in high schools?"

Her laughter swirled around him on the breeze. "No, I'm a counselor for troubled and runaway teens."

Not what he'd expected, but then, what had he expected? He yanked his thoughts away from Dixie—it was time to focus on the reason they were together. "Have you been inside?"

Shielding her eyes from the sun, Dixie turned to face the lodge. "I thought I'd wait for you, to be fair."

Jack kept his expression blank, though the admission surprised him. In his line of work, decent people were a rare commodity.

He stared at the two-story structure. A low porch wrapped around it to disappear around either side. The windows were dark and the door was a hand-carved, massive wooden panel.

Walking up the two hand-hewn steps to the porch, he looked closer at the door. "What is that supposed to be?"

"Well, I believe, it's a wolf and an elk intertwined and woven into a heart."

She stood close enough that her warmth seeped through the thin fabric of his shirtsleeve. "You see all that?" He stepped sideways into his own cooler space.

"Actually, no. The park ranger in town filled me in on the place." She wrapped her fingers around the wrought-iron door handle. "Ready?"

"Always." He followed when she pushed against the wooden panel.

Cool air spilled over the sill and greeted them. The air danced with dust, captured in the beams of sunlight filtering through the dirty windowpanes. The ceiling rose two stories high. Only two rockers furnished the massive room.

Dixie stared at the floor-to-ceiling moss rock fireplace visible against the farthest wall. In her mind's eye, she saw a fire crackling and popping inside the dark hearth as groups of young people filled the room, chatting and laughing.

She loved it.

Turning, Dixie caught a look on Jack's face that caused her heart to plummet. It was the same look that must have been on her face only seconds before.

He loved it, too.

Rats. Probably had a list of girlfriends a mile long he would parade through the lodge like some kind of backwoods bachelor pad.

"It has potential, doesn't it?" Dixie broke the silence.

He turned guarded eyes toward her. "With a lot of hard work and time."

Suddenly feeling small in the dimness of the room, Dixie ran her hand along the wall next to the door frame. There was no light switch.

"I guess electricity was too much to hope for." She avoided looking at the man as her feet carried her deeper inside the main room of the lodge.

"Makes it more authentic. Being this far from town, I would have been surprised to see electricity. A generator will have to be put in." Jack paused in front of the massive fireplace. "There's plenty of wood outside for heat and I packed a lantern."

Who did he think he was, talking as though the lodge was already his?

"I brought a lantern, too." She wasn't totally unprepared. "Sadie and I found a warm water spring on the other side of the meadow."

"That'll keep us clean and I brought drinking water...."

His voice faded as she wandered into the area off the main room. It was obviously the kitchen. A massive cast iron stove with three removable burner lids sat against the far wall. A rustic table commanded the center of the room, but only three mismatched chairs awaited occupants. With the two ancient rockers in the main room, that made six pieces of furniture so far.

"Let's look upstairs," Jack said from the doorway. "And hope there's more furniture. These floors don't look comfortable."

Dixie followed him up the wide staircase that hugged the wall opposite the main room's fireplace. Looking up, she nearly groaned aloud. Jack's bottom was on the perfect level for bum watching, if she wanted to. And she definitely did not.

Her gaze fixed on the muscles bunching under the fabric as he mounted each step. The black denim hugged and moved across his buttocks as...

Knock it off. Keep your mind on the main objective.

What was it? Oh, yeah—win the lodge and help kids who were depending on her. Right. All she had to do was pretend the man in front of her was a robot or something. No problem.

Jack stopped abruptly and she found herself pressed full-length against his back. With her nose against his shirt it was hard to convince herself he was a robot, all metal and wires, instead of warm flesh and blood.

The scent of his skin tantalized and teased her. Why couldn't the man exude a pungent odor rather than raw sensuality?

"Sorry, I didn't realize how close you were." He stepped away and motioned toward the rooms on the left. "Ladies choose first."

Shaking herself to remove the feel of his shirt from her face, she picked the closest room and pushed the door open. Hope soared—a narrow, wrought-iron bed with a ticking mattress offered a measure of comfort.

"Looks like we may not have to rough it on the floor after all." She turned toward the next door. "Your turn."

While she peeked into the two remaining rooms, he pushed the door open and paused in the doorway. She glanced at him. Why didn't he go in or say something? Easing carefully around Jack to minimize any physical contact, she looked into the room.

Her shoulders slumped. "Oh."

The only decent piece of furniture and it had to be a bed. And not another narrow twin bed, but a substantial wooden creation. The four carved corner posts stretched toward the ceiling like silent sentinels. White canvas covered the mattress.

"Looks like we'll have to toss for it." Dixie reached into her pocket for a coin.

Jack's hand on her arm stopped her. "You take it."

"Well I…thanks, but this bed is bigger—so you take it. It's only fair, you're bigger." Her gaze stayed locked on the bed as she pictured it bathed in firelight from the fireplace. In her mind, she pictured two indistinct forms whispering beneath the blankets. Dixie shook her head, images like that she could live without.

Wait a minute. Something about the room seemed strange. Dixie walked to the fireplace. Crouching on her heels, she peered inside. It had been designed to heat *both* rooms—she could see her bed in the next room beyond the grate.

Jack stood next to the bed and yanked the canvas

onto the floor. "Someone's been taking care of this room."

"How can you tell?"

He slapped the mattress with his hand. "No dust. Logs in the fireplace ready for a match. Why don't you check that trunk under the window. I'll get some fresh air in here."

How had he noticed those details so quickly? Locating a chest, she lifted the lid and caught her breath. "Linens." She pressed a lace-trimmed, white sheet to her nose. "And they're fresh, no musty smell. Mr. Granger?"

"Not likely—he barely knew how to get here. What else did that ranger tell you?" He strode to the window and worked the latch free. Pushing against the protesting frame, Jack opened it.

Soft pine-scented breezes swept the stale air from the room.

Dixie gathered an armload of linens and worked on making the bed. "The ranger mentioned the previous owner bought the place and was preparing it for his sweetheart. I guess that's where this bed fits into the story." She jerked her thoughts away from the idea of the room as a honeymoon suite. "Anyway, she left him and he swore no one would see this place if she wasn't here to share it with him."

Jack continued to stare out the window without moving. He didn't respond to her words.

Snapping the top sheet in the air, Dixie said, "The fellow boarded up the windows and lived like a hermit. He rarely went to town and never paid his taxes.

Finally, the state took the place for payment of back taxes, the radio station bought it, and here we are.'' She paused in straightening a wrinkle in the top sheet. Why in the world was she making *his* bed, anyway?

Still, he didn't respond. Why had he asked about the place if he was going to ignore her? The strong, silent type was one thing, rudeness another. She noticed a frown pulling at the corner of his mouth.

''Mr. Powers, are you listening?'' Dixie watched him as her mouth went dry. Maybe he was dangerous after all. Why hadn't she listened to Maggie and brought pepper spray?

''Didn't you mention Sadie is in heat?''

She hurried to the window and followed his gaze. Her heart sank. ''Good grief, what is *your* dog doing?''

''I think it's obvious.'' He glanced at her from beneath thick lashes. ''And I believe *your* dog is enjoying it.''

CHAPTER THREE

DIXIE gripped Jack's arm. "Make them stop. Now."

"At this point it's best to let them finish."

"But he can't—I have an appointment to have Sadie bred." Panic edged in on her.

"Spontaneous is usually better."

What did he mean by that? She jerked away from him as though he'd pinched her and her gaze swung to the bed before focusing on the man again.

What was wrong with her? His words were totally innocent and she was putting an intimate twist on everything he said. Oh, why couldn't she act the cool sophisticate instead of the maidenly spinster?

Seeming to notice her silence, Jack turned from the window and fixed her with a narrow-eyed gaze. "I'm going to unload my truck."

He left the room without even glancing toward the bed. So, it was only *her* overactive imagination. Turning from the window and the sight of Sadie's deflowering, she sighed.

It was only four days—she'd get through it. Then she'd win the lodge and rearrange her life in order to run it. Easy as pie, right?

Yeah, right. And Sadie was still a virgin.

Ignoring the rumble in his belly reminding him he'd missed breakfast, Jack carried three boxes into the

main room of the lodge. He listened to shuffling footsteps overhead, followed by the sound of doors opening and closing—Dixie was exploring.

Good. As long as she was upstairs—she wasn't
messing with his head. Of all the rotten luck he was
saddled with a Pollyanna for four days before he took
the lodge away from her.

No, he wasn't taking it away because it wasn't
hers. Though he hadn't even entered himself. It was
Emma's dream—he had to focus on that thought.
Then maybe he wouldn't notice that Dixie wasn't
wearing a bra.

Lord-a-mighty, he'd been hard-pressed to keep
from staring at the gentle sway beneath her shirt. And
when she'd raised her arms to spread the sheet on
the bed—man. What were the odds that the place
would have a bed built for two? Between the bed
and the dogs mating under the pines, Jack had barely
managed to conceal his wayward thoughts.

Powers, knock it off.

He'd have to ignore Dixie's obvious attempts to
distract him. With his guard up, it was less likely to
affect him when she tried to sweet-talk him into letting her have the place.

Dixie didn't understand how determined he was.
He had to win the lodge for Emma, no matter what.

Jack tried to keep his thoughts away from Dixie,
but it was useless. He wondered if Miss Sunshine
had the proper equipment to rough it for a few days.
April in the Rockies was a long way from warm. It

wasn't his problem…so why couldn't he turn off the inner voice telling him to check on the woman?

Listening for sounds of movement from downstairs, Dixie looked at where Sadie and Tigger lay dozing under the trees. All that was missing was the pro-verbial cigarette dangling between their canine lips. Satisfaction seemed to ooze from their fur, but then why shouldn't it? Total strangers less than thirty minutes ago, they were now intimately acquainted.

What am I going to tell the breeder?

And how could she stop envying her *dog* for pity's sake? So what if the pooch had twice the sex life Dixie did? Oh jeesh, where was Maggie when she needed to be slapped silly?

Turning away from the window, Dixie carefully avoided glancing toward the bed Jack would occupy as she left the room, closing the door behind her.

Moments later, she tucked the last blanket beneath the foot of the mattress on her smaller bed. Brushing her hair back from her face, she looked at the legs of the bed visible in the next room—maybe she should erect some sort of screen in front of the shared fireplace.

Then again, they were both adults. Not to mention they'd have to use the fireplace for heat once the sun dipped beyond the ridge of mountains to the west. Nightfall was approaching quickly. She had forgotten to worry about that aspect of the stay.

Four days stretched endlessly, especially with temptation visible behind a wall of red-hot flame.

"It'll be dark soon."

Dixie nearly dropped the pillow she'd been forcing into the cotton pillowcase. How did a man with so much muscle manage to sneak up on her? She stared at the armload of wood in Jack's arms.

He glanced toward the hearth. "I thought I'd put wood in both rooms, so whoever wakes up will be able to toss a log in." The muscles in his thighs strained against the fabric of his jeans as he crouched to stack the wood on the stone ledge.

Like she was going to get any sleep tonight. "Thanks. I picked up sandwiches in town if you're hungry."

"Sounds great."

The full strength of his gaze turned to her and she suffered severe brain dump. Heat raced up her neck and she pretended intense concentration on the task at hand. Never had a pillow required such personal attention.

After watching her for several seconds as though reading her wicked thoughts, Jack stood. "Does the double-sided fireplace bother you?"

Did she look as gauche as she felt? She shrugged, pretending an air of unconcern. "Not as much as the lack of indoor plumbing." *My, don't I sound the sophisticate?* Except for the almost imperceptible huskiness to her words.

One corner of his lips tipped upward and Jack sauntered through the door, presenting Dixie with another unobstructed view of his backside.

Phenomenal.

Groaning, she dropped onto the edge of the bed and clutched the pillow to her chest, hoping to slow the pounding of her heart.

Maybe Dixie should tell Jack how much she needed the lodge, how much the kids at the center needed a place like this. He couldn't possibly want the lodge for anything nearly as important. Dixie shook her head. It sounded goofy inside her head—verbalized it would be whining. And she didn't want him thinking she was using her feminine wiles to convince him to let her win.

No, she would not seduce the man just to win the lodge. As if she'd even know how. Perhaps her mother was right after all—Dixie needed to get out more. The verbal interplay between a man and a woman had her stumped with a capital "S."

Plumping the pillow as she put it in place, Dixie traced a delicate letter embroidered on the edge of the pillowcase. What did the "C" stand for and who had provided the clean linens?

Ah, well. It really didn't matter—Dixie was simply glad someone had thought of it.

The dogs yipped and barked. She moved down the stairs and toward the large front window. Scrubbing the pane with her sleeve, Dixie pressed her nose against the glass and smiled at the scene.

Jack balanced a box in his arms while the dogs bounded around him, and seemed to be attempting to start a game with the man. Tigger faked to the left and Sadie dashed after him.

Right between Jack's legs.

Dixie gasped, and then relaxed when he managed to remain upright thanks to his fast-footed shuffling. She pressed a hand against her chest to calm her thumping heartbeat. She knew part of her reaction was simply a reaction to watching Jack. The man was walking dynamite—why couldn't he be less of a temptation and more of a geek?

Because Jack was the furthest thing from a geek Dixie had seen in her life.

Maggie would have a field day with him. That was what Dixie needed—Maggie. Dixie's thoughts momentarily turned to the cellular phone in her car. Maybe she could sneak away for a quick call on how to act nonchalant when one was practically drooling over a man. No, her friend would spend the whole call laughing, and Dixie would be no better off than before.

Jack stepped onto the porch and she yanked herself back from the window. The last thing she needed was for him to think she was some kind of sex-starved, desperate woman lusting over him from inside the lodge. Because she wasn't, no matter what her mother said. It wasn't a crime to be single.

Dixie couldn't avoid the man all day. Taking a deep breath, she pulled the front door open and walked straight into Jack.

"Oomph." The box he'd been carrying tumbled onto the porch.

Strong hands steadied Dixie, and she tried to remember how to breathe as she met Jack's gaze. Humor and another unidentifiable emotion stared down at her from his eyes. A tightening caught her midsection as her breath paused.

"I'm s-sorry. I didn't see you." Wishing the moment would pass before she died of mortification, Dixie stepped out of his reach. She instantly missed the warmth of his touch.

Jack frowned, bending to retrieve his box. "No problem, I didn't see you, either."

Brushing past Jack, she hurried to unload her gear. As she unhooked the bungee cord from under the rusted bumper, Dixie slapped her hand on the left corner of the trunk lid while bumping her hip against the right side.

The lid sprang open—the method never failed. Dixie had a special relationship with her old car. Although friends constantly urged Dixie to invest in a more reliable vehicle, she couldn't do it. Loyalty counted for something. Besides, the car was paid for. And *that* counted for a lot.

Pulling her duffel bag onto the ground, she leaned in and lifted the box of supplies.

"I'll take that."

Startled, Dixie stared up at Jack. "How do you do that?" She surrendered the box into his large, capable hands. After all, it *was* heavy and she'd made his bed. Fair was fair.

Jack walked toward the lodge. "Do what?"

Jogging to keep up with his ground-eating stride, Dixie rephrased the question that had bothered her since they'd explored the upstairs. "You know, sneak up on me. Notice every little detail."

"I never sneak." Jack answered as he balanced the box.

"Oh, in the kitchen. Please." Dixie followed. "Well, not sneak, but you move quietly."

He placed the box on the table. "It's my job."

Visions of the type of jobs requiring stealthy movements raced through her mind, each worse than the one before. FBI agent, cat burglar, hired assassin, serial killer…

As though sensing her unease, Jack pulled his wallet out and flipped it open. He retrieved a business card and held it toward her.

Raising her chin to meet his gaze, Dixie took it. Jack Powers, Private Investigative Services, Discretion and Professionalism Our Trademark.

Oh. Well, how could she have known he was some kind of cop or something?

"Does that ease your mind?" Crossing his arms, he grinned revealing a dimple in the center of his chin.

Smiling back, Dixie ignored the heat pounding in her face and the urge to place the tip of a finger in that adorable dent below his lower lip. "You can't be too careful."

"I know. I tell Emma the same thing all the time."

I knew it.

Of course the man would have a woman waiting at home—Dixie had guessed that from the start. So why did she feel as though she'd swallowed a boulder the size of Colorado?

Watching Dixie as though he could read each

thought that crossed her features, Jack narrowed his eyes. "Emma is my secretary among other things."

"That's nice." An office romance—it wasn't surprising. Dixie knew she'd find the man distracting at work...or in a store...or anywhere, so why wouldn't his secretary?

Dixie filled the awkward silence by unloading the box. The skin at her nape tingled, a reminder that Jack stood near. And by her body's reaction, he watched her.

What was going through his mind?

Jack tried to control his wayward thoughts. He wouldn't think of Dixie as a tempting, attractive woman. It clouded his judgment and caused him to forget why he had to win the lodge. To take care of Emma. Everything he did over the next four days had to focus on that goal.

Dixie dropped a roll of paper towels and crawled under the table to retrieve it. The view she offered nearly made him groan aloud as he ran a hand down his face.

It was warm in the kitchen...or maybe it was just him.

Jack needed to get some air, and the tightening in his lower body told him the sooner, the better.

Turning to stare at the far wall, Jack tried to keep the strain of physical awareness from his voice. "I'm going to take Tigger for a walk. Where did you say you found the spring?"

Good, his voice betrayed none of his inner turmoil

or lust for the maddening woman. He risked a glance toward her.

"It's behind, no it's over, wait..." Dixie blew a strand of hair off her lower lip before nibbling the delicate skin with her teeth. She scuffed the toe of her shoe against the rough planks and avoided his gaze.

Oh, man. He headed for the door. "Never mind, I'll find it." And pull himself together while he was at it.

"Would you mind taking Sadie? I'll finish unpacking."

"No problem." Jack didn't look back.

Dixie stared at the spot where Jack had stood only moments before. The tension between them was becoming a problem. Maybe it was only a problem for her. He probably had no idea the paths her wayward thoughts traveled whenever they focused on him.

The last thing she'd do was let him see the effect he had on her...and her libido.

She really needed to get out more. The minute Dixie returned to Denver, she'd let Maggie set her up on a date. Heaven knew her friend had nagged her enough about the possibility. Right about now a blind date with a safe, boring office guy looked good...and safe compared to the fantasies she was entertaining about her rival.

Dixie wandered up the stairs with her duffel bag. Maybe if she unpacked it would take her mind off the thought of Jack sleeping in the next room, separated only by a wall of flickering flame.

Dumping her bag on the bed, she rummaged through the contents. Maggie had included a good assortment of clothing, but where were Dixie's new flannel pajamas? Dixie haphazardly tossed clothing aside. There was no way her friend could have missed the full-coverage, warm, fuzzy pajamas. She distinctly remembered laying them on her bed, right next to the duffel bag.

A gentle breeze from the open window playfully ruffled her hair. Unzipping the side pocket, she plunged her hand in and pulled the only remaining garment from the bag.

Oh, please, no. I'm going to kill Maggie. I'm going to torture her, then kill her. I'm going to pluck every hair from her head, torture, then kill her.

Dixie drew a shuddering breath, looked at the ceiling, counted to ten and then looked at the wisp of fabric in her hand.

Maggie wouldn't do this to her, would she? Staring at the scrap of white lace and silk that she shook out to reveal as a long gown, Dixie squeezed her eyes shut and reopened them. Yes, Maggie would do this. They'd been pulling pranks on each other for years, since middle school. Why should now be any different?

Because Dixie was alone with a man—a gorgeous, distracting man—in a remote mountain lodge. She needed her man-tailored, thick, matronly flannel pajamas. Not this frothy creation designed for seduction and quick removal.

Cramming the garment into the deepest corner of

her bag, Dixie grinned. Maggie thought she was *so* clever. Well, Dixie would simply sleep in her clothes. When she returned to her normal life she'd fill Maggie's shampoo bottle with hair remover.

Then they'd be even.

Jack tossed another stick ahead of the dogs. Scrambling to outrun each other, Tigger and Sadie each gripped an end of the stick in their mouths and jogged back toward him after fetching it.

A couple of Siamese twins joined at the jaw.

The two were already an item. How was Jack going to keep his mind off any type of involvement with Dixie if the dogs kept behaving like canine honeymooners? As if he even wanted to get to know the tiny dynamo any better.

The gentle swell of Dixie's soft voice drifted through his mind, a three-pound voice to go with a three-thousand-pound personality. A memorable combination.

Tigger nudged Jack's hand and pulled him back into the present. There in front of him, a cloud of steam crept over the ground from a small pool. The hot spring Dixie had mentioned.

So much for his powers of observation Dixie had mentioned earlier. If Tigger hadn't nudged him, Jack would have strolled right into the water.

"Good boy." Jack patted the top of Tigger's head. Obviously satisfied that he'd led his master somewhere, Tigger flopped onto the grass and rested his head on his paws. Sadie curled next to him and dozed.

Crouching at the water's edge, Jack tested it with his hand. It was definitely warm enough for bathing.

An image of Dixie emerging from the natural spring popped into his mind. Water streaming from her hair, nothing between her wet skin and the mountain air but a veil of steam, looking up at him through lashes spiked with moisture…

Whoa.

Jack groaned and shook his head. Staying far from the pool when Dixie used it would be imperative. If his body reacted this strongly to a mental image, the reaction in person would be nuclear.

That took care of the daylight hours, but what about the nights? Jack stared up through the branches of the aspen trees that ringed the pool. What if the woman slept as naked as he fantasized she swam?

The problem of the shared fireplace reared its head. He wasn't worried—Dixie seemed the sensible type. A set of flannel pajamas was probably the first thing she'd packed for the cool mountain nights.

Yeah, Jack was sure there would be no problem with the nights.

CHAPTER FOUR

DIXIE watched the light fade in the evening sky. The pines were silhouetted against the purples of the sunset, stark and proud.

Where were Jack and the dogs?

Carefully lighting her cantankerous lantern, she adjusted the knob until the mantel emitted a soft glow that dispelled some of the shadows that had begun to creep into the lodge. But it also created new ones.

Dixie wrapped the fleece jacket closer around her shoulders. Shadows didn't normally scare her, but it *was* a long way to town.

Why had she watched so many of those ridiculous slasher movies with her students? The videos had seemed stupid at the time, but alone in the woods, now they seemed possible. Rummaging in the cooler, Dixie pulled the deli sandwiches out and arranged them on paper plates. Chips completed the gourmet meal. Ha—at least Jack couldn't accuse her of trying to get him to surrender the lodge by plying him with home-cooked meals. Cooking was not one of her strong points.

She cooked almost as well as she packed and organized. Abominably.

Footsteps and playful barking sounded from the

front porch. Relief coursed through Dixie and she
relaxed the shoulders she hadn't realized were tense
as Jack strolled in.

It was nice to have someone else in the lodge, even
if that someone came through the door looking as
good as when he'd left.

Dixie glanced at Jack from under her lashes.
Correction—he looked even better than when he'd
left for the walk. With his hair mussed and the smell
of pine and mountain wind clinging to him, Jack was
temptation in the flesh. The image his collar turned
up against the chill gave sparked Dixie's imagination. He personified every bad boy Dixie's mother
had warned her about.

And heaven knew a woman couldn't resist a boy
who was considered edgy and dangerous. Much less
a man.

Ladies loved outlaws.

Across the space of the room, they stared at each
other in silence. Dixie shivered with awareness, not
from the coolness of the room.

What seemed like minutes, but was only seconds,
passed before Dixie broke eye contact and turned
away, motioning toward the kitchen.

"I have sandwiches." *Oh, good line, Dixie.*
Intelligent and to the point, kind of like, "You
Tarzan, me Jane."

Jack turned to the still-open front door and whistled. Tigger and Sadie bounded in and sat in front of
the man with adoring looks on their faces as Jack

pushed the door closed. Great, Dixie's dog had turned traitor for the competition.

Shrugging out of his jacket, Jack tossed it onto one of the rockers. Dixie stared at the pull of fabric across his chest, watched as muscle and sinew worked beneath skin scattered with dark hair on his outstretched arm. Didn't the man realize how distracting he was? Maybe that was part of his plan to steal her lodge, distract her to the point of insanity.

If she wasn't careful, it just might work.

"I'll get the fire going upstairs before we eat." Grabbing his lantern from the hearth, Jack took the stairs two at a time and quickly passed from sight on the landing.

Shaking her head to try to clear the interest she'd developed in the man, Dixie patted her thigh as she walked back to the kitchen. "Come on you two. Time for dinner."

She was starving. If Jack thought she'd wait for him to come downstairs before eating, he could think again. Her dinner was getting cold. Well, stale anyway.

The air that seeped down the flue as Jack turned the damper was musty. He hoped no birds had clogged the chimney with a nest.

Scraping a match across the stone hearth, he held it inside the fireplace. Satisfied when the smoke drifted upward, he shook out the flame and stacked kindling and wood shavings on the grate.

From his crouched position, Jack had a clear view

into the next room. The iron bed seemed closer than it had during daylight hours. He'd have to make sure he didn't stoop too low when he tossed a log on in the middle of the night. Otherwise he'd have an unobstructed view of Dixie, in bed, hopefully wearing full-coverage sleep clothes.

Touching a fresh matchstick to the stacked tinder, Jack nodded when it immediately caught. Replacing the fire screen, he stood. No sense in delaying the inevitable. It was time to go downstairs. Besides, if his snarling stomach was an indication, he was starved.

Wandering into the kitchen moments later, Jack surprised Dixie feeding a chip to Tigger. She turned pink while the idiot dog licked his chops.

"He looked hungry," Dixie defended.

Jack tried to ignore how the splashes of color on her face made her eyes look bigger. Swinging a chair backward, he straddled it and picked up his sandwich. "Tigger's a mooch. Thanks for dinner."

Smiling, she shrugged. "As you can tell, I worked on it all day. Did you find the spring?"

Jack nodded as he licked mustard from his fingertips. He caught a fresh blush stealing across her cheeks. Interesting—there weren't many people who blushed anymore. He found it refreshing.

"I thought we'd work on a schedule."

She raised her eyebrows. "For what?"

"The hot spring, when we should each use it." He liked the way confusion darkened the green in her eyes.

"Why...oh." Dixie sipped from her soda can as if to cover her embarrassment. "I hadn't thought of that. I'm up early, would you mind if I go first?"

"That's fine—I'll assume you're done by eight o'clock. Just be sure to make a lot of noise on your way to the pool." Jack put the last bite of sandwich into his mouth.

"You mean because of animals?"

"Do they scare you?" Maybe she'd hear a squirrel rustling in the trees and decide to leave before the time limit expired. The thought was no longer appealing. Jack didn't like the idea of Dixie scared. At all.

"Oh, no, I'll take Sadie with me." She glanced at her watch. "I'd better head upstairs. It's been a long day."

Jack watched as she stretched both arms above her head while she stood. The move accentuated the curves of her body and his tightened in response.

He nearly groaned aloud.

Looking at the far wall rather than Dixie, Jack focused on less intimate topics. "I closed the windows and the fire is fine for a while."

He'd give her time to settle in before he went up. No sense taking a chance on the woman running around in her pajamas, even if they were most likely safe and matronly.

Dixie dropped her plate and can into the makeshift trash bag. After a soft good-night in Jack's direction and lantern in hand, she escaped the heat of his penetrating gaze reflected in the soft glow of his lantern. Sadie padded along beside her.

It wasn't until she stepped inside her room and leaned against the closed door that Dixie allowed herself to relax. Her spine still tingled from the feel of Jack's stare as she'd left the kitchen. Maybe he was glaring daggers at her so she'd give up the lodge.

No way. After experiencing the beauty and seren-ity of the area, as well as the lodge itself, she was more convinced than ever that it would prove the perfect retreat for troubled teens. A place to get their heads together without the pressure from friends and family that usually only confused them more.

Glancing about the austere room, Dixie silently thanked Jack for the glow and warmth offered by the fire. After a moment spent absorbing the heat, she glanced at the clothes she'd worn all day and gri-maced. Evidence of her explorations was smeared on her sweatshirt and jeans. Grass stains, pine sap, and dirt mingled to form a wonderful design—if she were into walking abstract art.

Nothing sounded better than slipping into her snug, flannel pajamas and burrowing under the layers of lace-trimmed sheets and quilts on the antique bed. Why had Maggie picked now to pull another prank?

It was decision time—sleep in uncomfortable clothing or wear the lace creation Maggie packed for her. Chewing her already mangled thumbnail, Dixie eyed the fireplace then crouched in front of it.

Well, unless the man knelt in his room and pur-posely tried to focus on her, he wouldn't be able to see much. What were the odds he pictured her as a woman, much less a desirable one? He had Emma waiting for his return.

She'd go with the nightgown—it wasn't as though she planned to wander around the lodge. Just put it on, sleep, take it off and hide it. No problem.

Following a sponge bath from the pitcher of water she'd carried up earlier, Dixie yanked the gown from the bottom pocket of her bag. In the firelight, it seemed no more substantial than moonlight and twice as seductive.

The fabric slipped over her head and slithered downward. Smoothing it over her hips, she rubbed the fabric between her thumb and forefinger. Okay, it was soft. But that didn't make it the right attire for a rustic lodge. The front hem of the gown stopped against the top of her feet as the back trailed on the floor.

I look like a 1940's Hollywood starlet.

Glamorous or not, it was time for bed. Raising the hem of the gown as she walked, Dixie climbed between the pristine sheets and pulled them beneath her chin. After a moment's chill, her body warmed the fabric and she sighed. This was comfort, plain and simple. She'd have a good night's sleep and explore more of the surrounding woods in the morning.

Right after she made use of the hot spring.

Jack lowered the flame on his lantern to a barely visible glow and decided he'd given Dixie enough time. If she wasn't in bed and sleeping by now—too bad. He was tired and Tigger seemed to agree. The dog yawned widely as he followed Jack up the stairs.

Instinct from his years as a private detective compelled Jack to pause on the landing and listen for sounds of movement, both inside and outside the lodge. Nothing but a howling coyote and night sounds reached him.

Good, Dixie must be asleep. Not that it would bother him to run into the woman—she didn't affect him one way or another. Yeah, and Tigger wasn't a four-legged dog.

Closing his door with only a whisper of sound, Jack turned to the bed. Shadows cast by the flames made the posts appear to reach the ceiling. What had the man been thinking who'd carved it? Obviously he'd had long nights with his prospective bride in mind.

Jack replaced his shirt and jeans with shorts and a tank top. No sense taking a chance on giving Dixie a stroke by sleeping as he usually did.

Bending in front of the hearth, he stoked the glowing embers before carefully placing two logs on top. Careful to keep his gaze averted from Dixie's bed behind the crackling flames, Jack ran impatient fingers through his hair. He waited long enough for the logs to begin crackling and popping before turning away.

Tigger settled onto the floor next to the bed. After a couple of soft whines, the dog slipped into a deep sleep.

Jack wished falling asleep were that easy. Pick a

spot, spin around three times, and start snoring. It would certainly make life easier—especially tonight.

Pacing to the window, he focused on the silver bark of the moonlit aspens. Why was he allowing thoughts of Dixie to keep him awake? Her natural beauty, constant smile, not to mention nice curves, were an attractive combination. He should be able to shrug off the enticement, put it into a neat file and get on with winning the lodge. Emma was counting on him.

That was what mattered…Emma. Not getting to know Dixie, or fantasizing about tasting her lips. The lodge was his objective so he could take care of Emma as she'd taken care of him, nothing else.

Hell, it was useless. Sleep was a universe away. Long strides carried him to the door. Maybe a glass of water would take his mind off the competition in the next room.

Yanking the door open, Jack stopped as though he'd slammed into a wall. Dixie stood in the hallway. Wide-eyed and looking like pure seduction on a stick in a white, silky gown. She was obviously as surprised as he.

Sadie danced around her mistress.

In the dim light from his open door, Jack allowed his gaze to travel the length of Dixie's body. Forget drinking the glass of cold water, he'd simply pour it over his head.

Oh man, I'm in trouble.

Trouble—that's what Dixie saw in Jack's intense gaze. Even in the twilight of the lodge she could see that the gown hadn't gone unnoticed. Why couldn't Sadie have a bladder the size of a continent rather than the size of a butter bean?

Resisting the urge to cross her arms over her chest, Dixie cleared her throat. "Sadie needed to go out."

Jack's eyes narrowed. "Uh-huh."

Great, he probably thinks I'm traipsing around like this on purpose. Like she'd known he'd be awake and wandering around the lodge at this time of night. Dixie had listened for several minutes before venturing out of her room. And she'd still managed to run into him—could her luck get any worse?

"Nice gown."

Jack's smile caused the skin at the nape of her neck to tingle. Dixie willed her body not to respond to the smoky voice. "It's not mine."

Jack raised his eyebrows.

"I mean, I usually wear flannel…" She hated the heat that rose in her face as her words trailed away.

"I figured you for the flannel type."

What did he mean by that? As though she wouldn't wear a silk and lace creation. Jack Powers didn't know anything about her…okay, maybe he'd guessed correctly on her preference in pajamas, but Dixie didn't have to like his assumption.

"My friend, Maggie, packed for me. This—" she gestured toward the gown "—is her idea of a practical joke. It's all I have to sleep in." Dixie was babbling, but couldn't stop.

Jack nodded. "I like her sense of humor. Night." Stepping back into his room, he closed his door.

Dixie stared at the wooden panel. What had he meant? She glanced downward at herself. Had he liked the gown? Not that it mattered—she dressed to please herself. But she couldn't suppress the inner glow caused by the intensity of Jack's stare and his casual compliment.

Remembering the reason she'd ventured from her room in the first place, Dixie looked at Sadie wagging her tail whining. "Come on, Sadie. You started this with your bladder. Let's get you outside and finish it."

Several shivering minutes later, Dixie let Sadie in and escaped back into the privacy of her room. Lying in the bed, Dixie stared at the flickering flames and wondered if Jack was still awake.

No, she wasn't going to let this happen. An attraction to the man just didn't fit into her life. Dixie's job was too important to be distracted by hormones, and hadn't she learned about the reality of romantic relationships watching her mother's four disastrous marriages?

Turning onto her side, she punched the pillow into shape with her fist. Dixie refused to be attracted by a handsome face and tight physique. It was hormones and she could resist those. She'd been doing it all her life.

But the tightness in her stomach let her know otherwise. The hormones were gaining in the race for dominance over her brain.

Think about something else, Dixie, anything else.

The metric system.

Yeah, the metric system would do the trick. Hadn't the government been talking about converting to it for years? Trying to remember everything she knew about it took thirty whole seconds.

Darn, why hadn't she paid closer attention in Professor Blackwell's class? He'd warned them all that they'd regret not studying more. Maybe she'd drop him a note and let him know he'd been right. But, in all fairness, Professor Blackwell had never suggested the metric system as a way to get one's libido under control.

Not that it had even come close to working.

Squeezing her eyelids closed, Dixie willed sleep to come and morning to arrive. Everything would look better by the light of day. Especially when she was in jeans and a shirt rather than the nightgown provided by dear Maggie. Dixie would make her friend pay—big time.

Light peeked through the window and gently teased Dixie awake. Surprised at managing to doze off after contemplating a sleepless night, she stretched and gave a contented sigh. Early-morning sounds beckoned from beyond the closed window.

The trill of birds was accompanied by the gentle stirring of aspen leaves in the breeze. A natural symphony that outclassed anything the human world could produce.

It was time to use the natural hot spring and begin the day.

Listening for sounds of movement from the next room and hearing nothing Dixie quickly donned fresh jeans and a sweatshirt. She scooped the toiletry bag and towel into her arms and tiptoed down the stairs. Her leather moccasins were silent on the wooden treads and Sadie's claws made only gentle clicking noises.

Carefully closing the front door behind them, Dixie followed as Sadie led the way down the over-grown path. Minutes later, Dixie stood at the edge of the spring. Ten feet round, it glistened in the first light offered by the newborn sun. A soft mist rose from the surface and seemed to beckon her to enter the water, to slide into the welcoming warmth. The pool was surrounded on three sides by pine trees, their heady aroma added to the peaceful ambiance.

Heaven on earth.

After relishing the serene atmosphere for a mo-ment and glancing around, Dixie slipped out of her clothes, wrapped herself in the towel and tucked it above her breasts to keep it from sliding off. The brisk morning air raised gooseflesh on her exposed skin. Stepping gingerly on the slick rocks, she stepped into the water.

"Ahh…"

As the water level rose on Dixie's legs, she eased into the warmth and tossed the towel on top of her pile of clothing. In the center of the pool, she could touch bottom and be covered by the caressing water to her neck. Bliss.

Scrubbing her skin with a bar of environmentally safe, scented soap, Dixie glanced about for Sadie. She was nowhere in sight. The dog obviously had better plans than to sit and wait for her. Dixie couldn't blame her. And she knew Sadie wouldn't go far.

With a quick plunge, Dixie submerged her head then slicked the hair from her face and poured a measure of shampoo into her palm. The gentle motion of cleansing her hair both lulled and soothed. She closed her eyes and absorbed the sensations. Warm water, chilly where the air brushed her shoulders, lazy flies buzzing, nature-scented breezes, and the scurry of little feet in the undergrowth.

Dixie rinsed the shampoo from her hair, pausing to listen. There it was again—a scratching of tiny claws under the bushes and trees. She glanced into the greenery edging the pool. Nothing. Finally, glancing over her shoulder toward the spot she'd entered the water Dixie froze.

Oh, no.

Curled atop her neat stack of clothing and the towel lay a tiny skunk. It seemed to be sound asleep and in no great hurry to move. The warmth from her clothing must have attracted it.

Don't panic.

Dixie could hear a little voice inside her head telling her to breathe. Calmness was a definite plus in a crazy situation like this.

But how was she supposed to get out of the water and dressed? If she shouted, Jack would come running or the skunk would spray everything in sight with its foul, scented glands in defense, including her clothes. And Dixie couldn't just slip out of the water and saunter back to the lodge. Naked.

It was a lose-lose situation.

CHAPTER FIVE

JACK checked his watch. Again. It had been over an hour since Dixie walked past his bedroom door. She should have returned from the spring by now. Maybe she was higher maintenance than he'd thought.

Or maybe she'd drowned. The spring hadn't looked very deep, but maybe she'd slipped and hit her head.

Okay Jack—cool it.

There was a simple explanation. Letting his imagination run wild wasn't an option, not when he'd built his reputation on his levelheadedness and ability to think rationally in critical situations.

So, what was his next step?

Jack would just stroll on down to the spring. Casual. Not showing he was concerned. Tigger needed to go out anyway.

Dixie was probably picking wildflowers or taking the long way back to the lodge. After he located her, he'd head down and make use of the spring.

No problem. So why did his gut have that familiar twist as his instincts kicked in?

Something wasn't right.

The last bend in the trail lay ahead—Jack paused and listened. Nothing but silence greeted him. He glanced back and noticed Tigger had disappeared—

probably making friends with the neighborhood squirrels.

"Dixie." Jack spoke in a normal tone. It carried easily in the quiet trees, but there was no answer. "Dixie?" He called louder.

"Shhhhh." The soft hiss came from the direction of the spring.

What was the woman up to?

Moving closer, but still out of sight, Jack stopped. "Everything okay?"

Her whispered reply sounded strained. "I need help."

Jack moved closer, stirring the underbrush.

"Wait. Walk slowly or you'll startle it." Her *words* carried urgency.

What had Dixie stumbled into? He only hoped it wasn't a snake, he could handle *anything* but a snake. Jack decided to stop guessing and discover what was going on for himself. He cautiously stepped from behind the screen of trees.

No way.

Quickly assessing the situation, Jack shook his head. A bad guy he could have handled. A fallen tree branch would have been a piece of cake. Big Foot, bring him on. But, what was he supposed to do with a skunk?

Dixie motioned with one hand, careful to keep the rest of her body below the water's surface. "There's a skunk," she whispered.

"Obviously." The furry body with its distinctive

stripe lying atop Dixie's clothing could be nothing else. "Why is it hanging around?"

One smooth shoulder peeked above the misty surface of the spring as Dixie shrugged. "If I knew, I wouldn't be trapped. Maybe it's young and doesn't know to be afraid of us. Or, maybe it's deaf." Her features softened into a gentle smile. "The poor thing."

"That *poor* thing packs a nasty defense spray." Jack chuckled. "How did you plan to retrieve your clothing?" He liked the situation more every second.

"If I'd figured that out, I wouldn't need help." Her eyes widened. "Please?"

Jack considered his choices. Everything pointed to removing the skunk. And he didn't like that option.

"Your shirt," Dixie whispered.

Ah, smart lady. Then he wouldn't have to tangle with the animal.

"Right." Jack pulled the T-shirt out of the waistband of his jeans and over his head. He held it toward her.

Dixie raised an eyebrow. "If you'll put it there—" she motioned toward the closest bush "—and turn around."

Jack grinned. What if he refused? Would she boldly rise from the steamy water and take the shirt from his outstretched hand?

Dixie frowned. Was Jack bluffing? Did she have the guts to step from the spring, bold and brash, to take the shirt from his fingers? No, she knew she didn't. But goodness knew she was tempted.

Sunlight streamed through the branches and highlighted Jack's muscled chest with interesting and mysterious shadows. His dark hair, intense gaze and jaunty grin caused her breath to catch in her throat. There it stuck, lodged behind a lump of raw desire.

Why couldn't she be sassy enough to call his bluff? Once in her life Dixie wanted to push the boundaries and test the water...just not today. And not completely naked.

As if he sensed her discomfort, Jack tossed the shirt onto the appointed bush and turned to face the trees. But he didn't move away.

Dixie stumbled two steps toward the shore. Another step and she'd be bared above the waist—she took two. Following the caressing warmth of the water, the morning air swept across her exposed flesh, raising chill bumps, as she scrambled the last few steps to the shirt.

The moisture on her skin hindered her efforts as she pulled the shirt over her head and shimmied it down her torso. Stopping at midthigh, the shirt did not offer as much coverage as Dixie would have liked, but it beat streaking back to the lodge.

Smoothing the fabric over her hips, Dixie glanced up and discovered Jack's gaze fixed on her chest. His intense stare caused her breasts to tighten and push against the damp shirt. She willed herself to meet his gaze.

A muscle leaped in Jack's temple and his eyes

darkened. He allowed his gaze to meander upward until their eyes locked.

Dixie swallowed, not allowing herself to follow the instinct to look away from the desire she saw burning in the blue depths of his eyes. A desire that reflected her own.

Jack held his hand toward her and she jumped.

"It's only a hand—you'll need help walking on the rough ground." He nodded toward her bare feet. "I'm afraid my shoes won't fit you."

"Oh." Dixie wished the telltale heat of embarrassment from her face. How had she mistaken concern for her feet for fierce passion? She placed her trembling fingers against the heat of his open palm and sensed an echoing tremble.

Jack slowly enfolded her fingers within his, gently laying each one atop her skin until her smaller hand was enveloped in his. "You're shaking, are you cold?"

Dixie knew she could lie, but what was the point? "No, I'm not cold."

At his soft intake of breath, Dixie thrust her chin forward. Scared or not, she'd pretend a boldness she was far from feeling. Hadn't she decided she was tired of life passing while thumbing its nose at her?

Jack reached forward and traced a finger down her cheek. "If you're not cold, why are you shaking?"

This was it, the moment of truth. It was time to make one of those pivotal decisions in her life. Dixie sensed Maggie behind her, prodding her forward.

Okay, Dixie could do this—be honest and let the man know how he affected her.

Dixie took a deep breath. "I'm afraid."

Jack frowned, evidently surprised by her answer. "Of me?"

Dixie took half a step closer. "No—afraid I don't have the nerve to kiss you. And more afraid you won't want me to."

Jack used both hands to frame her face. "You don't need to be afraid of me," he said as he brushed a thumb across her lower lip.

Somehow, Dixie had sensed this, but hearing him speak the words made it feel concrete. Made it all right to act on her instincts.

Rather than waiting as he lowered his face toward her, Dixie rose on her toes and met him halfway.

At the first taste of his lips, she sighed. Nothing prepared her for the exquisite ache caused by the sensation of his tongue sweeping across her teeth, seeking entrance. Willingly, Dixie opened to him and answered his search with one of her own.

Dixie closed the remaining inches between them and savored the hardness of Jack's chest against her softer curves. She raised her hands to his nape and brushed her fingertips through the soft hair curling against his warm skin.

With a groan, Jack traced a line from the back of her neck to the small of her back with his large hands. Awareness rippled, palpable and real—accentuating every taste and touch.

Jack eased back and rested his forehead against

hers. His breathing deepened and Dixie felt his heart-beats through the fabric. They echoed her own.

Running his right hand over her hip and upward, he rested it below her breast. "You know where this is heading?"

Still running on pure sensation, Dixie drew a cleansing breath to help her focus on Jack's words. "Where are we going?" His words didn't make sense. Did he want to go back to the lodge? Now?

"If we continue, we'll end up making love on the ground." His fingertips seared through the shirt.

Reality slammed into Dixie with all the finesse of a bull elk in full rut. Jack must think she'd been painted with the easy brush when they passed out libidos.

She dropped her hands to her sides as though he'd turned into a red-hot coal, which in basic terms he had. Hot and scorching to her peace of mind. "I can't..."

Jack lowered his hand to her hip. "Because..."

Dixie frantically searched her muddled brain for a reason that wouldn't categorize her as an idiot. Why *couldn't* she make love with this gorgeous man beneath the sheltering branches of the aspens?

"Engaged? Yeah, I'm engaged." She curled the fingers of her left hand inside her palm to hide her ringless finger. "To be married."

Jack removed his hand from her hip and stepped away. "That's normally what engaged means."

Dixie disliked misleading him, but the magnitude of what might have happened clouded her normally reasonable mind. The emotional, purely female side wrestled for control. "His name's…Guy, um…Guy Montgomery." She named a cocounselor at the center. Jack didn't need to know the man was in his sixties and happily married.

"He's a lucky man." Drawing a deep breath, Jack ran his fingers through the hair she'd so recently disheveled. "Let's get you back to the lodge, we'll come back for your things later."

They turned to look at the clothing at the same time and Dixie softly laughed. While they'd been distracted, the skunk had wandered away. As though his sole purpose had been to force she and Jack into the intimate embrace.

With the taste of the shared kisses with Jack on her lips, Dixie sent a silent thanks to the furry interloper. "At least I'll be able to wear my shoes now."

Several moments later, Dixie led the way along the path. The crunch of footsteps reminded her Jack was only a couple of steps behind. As if she needed a reminder, every time the shirt brushed against the back of her thighs it felt as though Jack reached out and touched her.

I'm losing it.

The walk that had taken only fifteen minutes earlier, seemed to last hours. Neither talked and Dixie didn't know how to break the awkward silence. Anything that popped to mind appeared too trivial in light of the passionate kisses they'd shared.

"Why do you want to win the lodge?"

Jack's question startled her. She stopped and turned. "Pardon me?"

"Is there any particular reason you'd want to live in such a remote place, or do you plan to sell the lodge if you win?" Jack moved around her and continued on the path.

Moving into step behind him, Dixie pondered his question. "I'd never sell." She didn't feel comfortable sharing her heart and the place she hoped to create for teens if she won. "What are you hoping to do with it if you win?"

"I guess Emma and I will figure it out after I win."

Dixie sensed a change in Jack at the mention of Emma.

They stopped in front of the lodge and Dixie cleared her throat. "You care a lot about Emma, don't you?"

Jack grinned. "I do."

Again, her stomach felt as though it were free-falling as Dixie met his gaze. The distant thunder of an airplane thousands of feet above the earth was a slash of reality in the surreal moment. How many more days did she have to get through?

Breaking eye contact, Dixie turned to the porch. "I'll go change and get your shirt back to you."

"No hurry, I have others." He turned back to the path. "Besides, it looks better on you. I'm going to use the spring." He strode away and disappeared.

Dixie gazed at the spot where he'd slipped into the trees and shook her head. The man paid her a compliment and she couldn't even speak. Ha, as if she'd know what to say. Maggie was the queen of the quick comebacks. Why hadn't Dixie paid more attention when her friend lectured on how to talk to the male of the species? Because it didn't matter—she had a goal. And it wasn't to snag a man—Dixie had a lodge to win.

All she had to do was convince her libido.

Jack ducked under the water's surface and rinsed the soap from his skin. Pushing his hair back with both hands, he floated in the warm water and stared at the patches of blue sky visible through the branches.

What had he been thinking to kiss Dixie? Especially without checking to see if she was involved with someone else first. Jack didn't mess with taken women, married or engaged—it was the same thing.

He saw enough infidelity in his line of work, Jack didn't want to end up in a place both he and Dixie would later regret.

Tigger and Sadie crashed through the underbrush and jumped into the water before Jack could find footing. Spitting out a mouthful of water, he grappled with the overgrown, canine kids before tossing a stick. "Go get it, you thugs."

Both dogs scrambled ashore and gave chase. Jack took advantage of their game and hurried to his clothing. Luckily no skunk had taken it upon himself to sneak a nap on them. Of course, Jack's clothing didn't smell like Dixie's. He didn't blame the critter for preferring the light flowery scent that seemed to cling to the woman. Jack did.

It didn't matter what she smelled like—Dixie was strictly off-limits. With only three days left until the contest ended, Jack figured he'd be okay. He had full control of his hormones…as long as he didn't look directly at the woman, or hear her laugh, or catch a whiff of her light, floral scent, or brush against her, or…

Hell, who was he kidding? This was going to be the longest three days of his life.

"Come on, guys." Jack whistled and the dogs raced to his side, each with an end of the stick he'd tossed in their mouths. If they hadn't looked like something from a Three Stooges skit, he'd separate them. Let them figure out how to get back connected by the stick.

As he approached the lodge, Jack heard the sound of metal banging against metal. What in the world was going on? He stopped short at the sight of Dixie on the porch steps chiseling something from the inside of a pan. Chunks of unidentifiable blackened goop flew from the end of a spatula. Some hit the trees and stuck, others plopped onto the dirt at her feet.

Noticing his arrival, Dixie shrugged and held the pan so he could view the contents. "Now you know, I'm not a cook. This was breakfast."

Jack leaned closer and detected the smell of charred food. "What was it, before you killed it?"

"Oatmeal."

Thank God, she'd burned it. He didn't have the heart to tell her he hated the noxious stuff, burned or otherwise. Each of the dogs sniffed the remains on the ground and retreated back to the shared stick.

"How about I put something together for us." Jack edged around the mess in the dirt.

Dixie smiled. "Would you…I mean did you bring breakfast food with you?"

Dazzled by the full potency of her smile, Jack spent a moment rearranging words in his head before he opened his mouth and tried to form a coherent sentence. "Emma packed the food, so I'm sure there's something we can work with."

"Great, you cook I'll clean up." Dixie glanced toward the pan she'd placed on the porch step. "As long as you don't turn it into charcoal."

Resisting the urge to offer her his hand, Jack walked up the steps and held the door open. "Let's see what I can do."

Twenty minutes later, Dixie was kneading dough for biscuits while he supervised. With flour on the tip of her nose and most other exposed parts of her body, she looked like an eager child. Well, an eager child with adult curves.

Jack rummaged in the cooler hoping the ice would cool his body's interest in Dixie. No such luck, but he did find breakfast sausage. He was lucky he'd let Emma pack for him without an argument. There was enough food for three weeks, much less three days.

Shrill ringing yanked him from his thoughts. Dixie jumped, spreading flour on the floor.

Jack looked around the kitchen. "What is that?"

Dixie nodded toward her purse on the far counter. "My cell phone. I didn't realize we'd have coverage out here. Would you mind answering it?" She raised dough-covered hands.

Tossing the sausage onto the table, he managed to retrieve the phone and push Talk by the fourth ring.

"Hello."

"Who's this?" A woman's voice demanded. "Where's my daughter? Who are you? Why are you answering this phone?"

Taking advantage of the woman's need to come up for air before she could continue, Jack spoke. "Ma'am. This is Jack Powers. Dixie is making biscuits."

Silence seemed to scream through the phone.

"Ma'am? Are you there?"

"Dixie is making biscuits?" Disbelief was in the woman's voice.

Jack grinned. "Well, I'm supervising."

"Oh, good. Then you must be that new boyfriend she told me all about. Chad, right?" The melodic voice tinkled with soft laughter.

If Dixie was engaged to a man named Guy, who was her mother talking about? "No, it's Jack."

"Oh…" Dixie's mother sighed. "Well, Chad didn't last long. But if you can teach her to cook, I like you already."

Jack shook his head at Dixie's raised eyebrows. He felt like he'd come in on the middle of an Abbott and Costello skit, totally confused but with an urge to grin.

"I'm Estelle. We are going to be great friends." Confidence rang in Estelle's words.

"Yes, ma'am." It was best to play along with delusional people—Jack had learned that long ago.

Wiping her hands, Dixie held her hand out for the phone. The color was high on her cheeks as she worried her full lower lip with her teeth.

Jack relinquished the phone and leaned against the counter.

Dixie held it to her ear. "Hi, Mom. No, he's not my boyfriend."

She listened and nodded. "In a lodge—outside of Pagosa Springs. Part of that radio contest I told you about. I kind of won.

"Yes, we're alone. No, he's perfectly safe. Because he told me he wasn't a serial killer. I thought of that, Mother."

Feeling slightly guilty about eavesdropping, Jack walked into the great room. Dixie's voice faded to a soft mumble.

Had Dixie lied about having a fiancé? Wouldn't her mother know who the man in her life was? He pondered the possibilities for a moment before a smile tipped his mouth. Could Dixie have been covering herself—it was the only reasonable explanation. After their kiss, she'd panicked, perhaps worried about being in such a remote location with him. After all, what did she really know about him? No more than he knew about her…and that wasn't much.

That, or it was as simple as the lady being engaged.

Footsteps sounded from the kitchen and Dixie walked into the room, empty-handed. Uncertainty seemed to show in her hesitant steps and gaze that met his through her lashes. Pushing his hands into his pockets, Jack resisted the urge to smile. "So, tell me more about Guy. When's the wedding? And who is Chad?"

CHAPTER SIX

DIXIE stared at Jack, not sure what wedding he was talking about. Oh, yeah, *her* wedding. Heaven only knew what her mother might have said to Jack when he'd answered her phone.

"Um…we haven't set a date yet. Chad was someone I dated last year, Mother gets names confused sometimes." She stumbled over the evasive words. Why couldn't Jack drop the subject? Dixie already felt bad enough about lying in the first place, she didn't want to heap more on top of it. The guilt would take years of therapy to assuage.

Seemingly unconcerned with her answer, Jack crouched and rubbed Tigger's ears. Sadie pushed closer to garner her share of the attention.

Kids probably like the man, too.

How was Dixie supposed to fight her growing attraction when he was so irresistible?

Dixie determined the truth wasn't an option right now, not when she was so attracted to Jack. Lying simply left a rotten taste in her mouth. She hated it.

She stared at her clenched hands, unable to meet Jack's gaze.

"Good."

Startled by the unexpected reaction, Dixie stared

at him. The grin on his face emphasized the dimple in his chin.

She cleared her throat. "Wh...why good?"

Jack stood and closed the distance between them with two strides. "You haven't set a date and your mother doesn't remember poor Guy's name."

Her heart flip-flopped. "So?"

Without looking away, he continued. "Are you in love with your fiancé?"

Resolutely, Dixie held her ground. She might as well confess everything. "I would never get engaged unless I were madly in love." There, at least that much was true. The lump in her throat grew larger.

He traced the line of her jaw with his finger. "You were scared by the kiss we shared." It was a statement.

At least he'd changed the direction of his questions, having to continue the charade of an engagement was twisting Dixie inside. There was nothing to deny—she gave a small nod. Great, her inexperience must have been blazingly obvious. Why hadn't she dated more? Because she was always working and had never regretted it before today.

Maggie had warned her that experience was the best teacher, simply reading about long, slow, wet, kisses in romance novels hadn't taught Dixie the finer points of real-life kissing. Not to mention the kisses she'd had from men in the past had come nowhere near the heat of those she'd shared with this man.

Jack replaced his finger with his open hand against

her cheek. She watched his gaze darken as he focused on her mouth—Dixie moistened her suddenly dry lips with the tip of her tongue.

Decision time, jump into real life or hide behind her uncertainty and career.

"You're engaged, this breaks all of my rules." Jack gave her the opportunity to draw back.

Drawing a shuddering breath, Dixie stopped thinking and analyzing. It was time to act. She grasped the wrist of his upraised arm and pulled his hand to her lips. A soft kiss placed on the palm of his hand produced a moan from the man watching her through half-lowered lids.

Encouraged by his spontaneous reaction, Dixie pulled the tip of one finger between her lips. She drew it deeper until it rested atop her tongue. Jack's sharp intake of air assured her that instinct was driving her in the right direction.

"You're playing with fire." Jack moved closer and brushed his knee against her thigh.

Slowly sliding his finger out of her mouth, she stared up at him. "I know." Dixie willed her smile to remain steady. He didn't need to know she trembled inside.

A whisper of movement brought her against the hard planes of his body. Tentatively Dixie pressed a hand to his chest. The pounding beneath her hand matched Dixie's own frantic heartbeat.

Thank heavens his passion seemed to match the desire reducing her limbs to molten flesh. Dixie knew she could no more step away from this moment than stop her next breath. There was no place else she'd rather be than with this man. In this moment.

Yesterday no longer existed with its warnings and fears. The future was beyond her view, but the present belonged to her if she dared grasp it. Dixie could wade in the shallows or plunge into the deep end and wet her entire body.

She allowed her eyelids to shut and hoped to avoid a belly flop on the waters of passion. At least she'd know one way or the other by taking a dip.

Jack didn't keep her in limbo. He pressed his lips to hers and brushed from side to side. The motion set an ache deep within her. An ache Dixie knew only he could satisfy. Moaning, she eased closer, seeking the heat offered. Seeking something just beyond the realm of her experience.

With a gentleness that seemed incongruous for such large hands, Jack cupped her face and deepened the kiss. Dixie sighed and raised on tiptoe to better reach his lips. A slight tip of her head allowed full contact with the mouth that was both breathtakingly firm and, yet, soft as the mist from the hot spring.

Jack bent his knees to reduce the disparity in their heights. Despite the difference, their bodies meshed and fit. Her softer curves finding just the right places against his angular build—like the pieces of a puzzle.

Worries about the crisis center, her mother's marriages, her fake engagement and everything outside of the moment disappeared. Dixie's world reduced to this one man—this one kiss.

Dixie wriggled her arms to free her hands pinned

between their bodies. She raised her fingertips to the back of Jack's neck and tentatively touched the satiny skin. Emboldened, she slipped her fingers into the hair that had teased her with its midnight depths. It was as soft as she'd imagined. The sensual pull of the strands on her skin tugged at a place deep within, pulled her more deeply into the intimate embrace.

Jack stroked the slope of her lower back, molding her closer. Dixie didn't believe they could strain nearer, but they managed.

Slow-paced, exploratory kisses deepened. She gasped at the frantic need rising inside. Their breaths raced and mingled, with one hand again resting against his chest she could feel his heartbeat.

Dixie moaned as a nudge against the back of her knee nearly caused her leg to give out. How had Jack lowered his hand to her knee?

The nudge came again, stronger this time. With the way she trembled, Dixie feared the next push would cause her spaghettilike legs to collapse.

Pulling only a breath away from Jack's lips, she raised heavy eyelids to search his expression. He watched her with passion-darkened eyes, seeming to question why she'd stopped.

Dixie cleared her throat before words could slip past her lips. ''Why did you do that?''

''Why did I kiss you when I know I shouldn't?'' Jack's voice was low and husky.

''No,'' she whispered, feeling awkward. ''Why did you bump the back of my leg?'' Maybe it was a

lovemaking technique she'd never heard of, much
less attempted.

"Honey, both of my hands are touching your back
and my legs are holding me up." He grinned. "Unless I have an extra appendage I'm not aware of, all
of my limbs are accounted for."

Feeling foolish on top of awkward, Dixie willed
the heat from her face. Easing back another inch, she
twisted her neck and looked to where she'd felt the
nudge.

Sadie stared up at her.

What rotten timing, but seeing the prize held
gently in the dog's mouth, Dixie understood. Sadie
had made a new friend and wanted to brag.

Dixie forced herself to shyly meet Jack's curious
gaze. "Mystery solved."

"Oh?"

"Sadie found a playmate and wants to share." She
stepped sideways to offer Jack a view of the adorable
twosome.

"For the love of—" Jack moved two steps away
from the dog.

His tone displayed none of the humor she'd expected. If Dixie didn't know better, she'd think the
man was nervous. Dixie glanced toward Sadie and
the small snake dangling, unharmed, from her mouth.

"Don't worry, she never hurts them." Bending,
she scratched Sadie's head. "Good girl, I'm proud
of you. Is this your new friend?

"Give." Placing her hand below the snake, Dixie

waited. Sadie obediently allowed the snake to slip out of her mouth.

Dixie straightened and held the snake up for Jack to inspect.

I can't believe it.

Jack had backed another ten feet while she'd retrieved the snake. The set of his shoulders and grim expression told her he was not pleased.

"She honestly didn't hurt it."

He didn't move closer. "Is it poisonous?"

"It's harmless, good for keeping the bug population under control." A sneaking suspicion slipped into her mind. "Snakes bother you, don't they?"

Jack waited so long to answer, Dixie thought he'd decided to ignore her question.

"Okay, they're my Achilles' heel." He tipped his head to one side. "Not too many snakes in the city."

Dixie repressed the smile threatening to slip out. Somehow, Jack's confession made her feel less vulnerable, closer to him. She, with her fear of a romantic entanglement, wasn't the only one with an irrational fear.

Rather than press the issue and attempt to make a reptile lover of the man, Dixie carried the snake outside.

An irrational fear needed time and patience—not to mention the right person and setting—to be conquered.

Walking outside into the sunlight, she released the small creature into the grass. It wiggled and disappeared into the dense foliage.

Dixie glanced back toward the lodge. Jack stood framed in the doorway. The air left her lungs and an ache settled itself in the vicinity of her heart. She realized she'd found the right person and the perfect setting. Now, all she had to do was take that final step and conquer the fear.

Could she do it? Could she offer her heart and trust that this man would treat it gently? Fear and desire tumbled about in her stomach.

Jack watched as Dixie gently placed the snake on the ground. The sun turned her hair to dark gold. His fingers burned with the need to bury themselves in the tempting length.

Unfortunately the earlier passionate moment had dissipated with the appearance of the evil serpent. Harmless or not, Jack didn't like the slimy things. Sure did put a dent in a guy's ego, though, to have to admit a weakness.

Dixie stood and faced the lodge. Backlit, each curve of her body was accentuated. She raised a hand and brushed the hair from her eyes.

Jack's body tightened. The woman represented Eve in the garden, consorting with the snake to plot his downfall. And urging him to take a bite of temptation. Lush, juicy, temptation.

He couldn't remember all of the logical reasons he shouldn't touch Dixie or taste her sweet mouth again. Where was his willpower when he needed it? Evidently it had gone south with the majority of his blood flow.

The woman was engaged.

But not married, Jack. Yet.

Their gazes locked. Dixie's lips parted slightly as though she too was reliving the kisses they'd shared. It was going to happen—the certainty raced between them on a current of pure electricity. No longer was there a question of "if." It was a matter of when.

Jack shook his head to clear the images the thought evoked. Giving a low whistle, he stepped outside as the dogs raced toward him.

"I'll take them for a run." Jack followed the dogs into the trees without looking back.

If he risked looking at the woman again, it would happen now. The passion simmered too close to the surface. All it would take was the slightest breath of air to fan it into flames, red-hot and searing flames.

The sound of soft footsteps on the porch alerted him to when Dixie turned and entered the lodge. Knowing she was inside did nothing to ease the tension in his muscles. Jack felt she still watched him.

Dixie stood in the deep shadows of the great room and watched through the smudged windowpane as Jack disappeared into the pines. Even out of sight, the memory of his heavy-lidded eyes gazing down at her following their heated kisses, haunted her.

If only the specter of the mysterious Emma wasn't there to bring a guilt Dixie didn't like. What if Jack and Emma had an understanding, were a committed couple? What now?

A line had been crossed. Dixie wasn't sure when

she'd stepped over it, but she wasn't going back. She couldn't.

Maggie had always told her this time would come. The time when her heart, mind, and body would know when she'd met the man who could help her forget her fears. A time when the desire would overshadow the doubts.

Jack was the man.

This was the time.

But what about Emma?

Turning away from the window, Dixie pressed a hand to her stomach. If it was the right man and the right time, why did she feel like throwing up?

Maybe Maggie had an answer for that, too.

CHAPTER SEVEN

"WHAT do you mean you don't know if he has protection?" Maggie's outraged voice blasted through the cell phone.

Dixie shook her head, even though her friend couldn't see her. "It's not as though I planned this."

"Honey, weren't you a Girl Scout, or something?"

"Yes, but—"

"No, buts. Good grief, you're twenty-seven." Maggie sighed. "Didn't your mother give you *the talk* years ago?"

"Mag, this isn't helping. I just want to know if it's normal to feel like I have food poisoning?"

"Girl, you have it bad." Laughter punctuated the words.

Dixie frowned. "Food poisoning?"

Maggie's rich laughter carried on invisible sound waves. "A crush, heartthrob, decadent desire... whatever you want to call it. You've got it bad."

"But, I didn't plan this." Dixie plopped onto the large rocker next to the fireplace. "I was going to wait until my thirties before I started thinking about romance."

"Looks like romance has other plans, no sense fighting fate."

"But, Maggie—"

"Stop thinking and analyzing—enjoy the stomachache and everything that goes with it."

Dixie set the chair in motion with the tip of her shoe against the scarred pine floor. "I'll try."

"One last thing."

Now what. "What's that?"

"If he hurts your heart, I'll twist him like a pretzel." Determination and a protective tone gave the words bite.

Dixie knew she meant it. "Thanks. You're the best."

"Now, hang up, this is costing you a small fortune."

"Bye." Hitting the power button, Dixie laid her head back and closed her eyes. Fortune or not, hearing Maggie's voice was worth every cent. A bit of reality in the middle of an unreal situation.

The reassurance and caring from her friend had settled some of the butterflies wrestling around in her stomach. Some, but not all. It was easy to talk big to Maggie, especially when her friend couldn't see the way Dixie's hands trembled. She had a feeling Maggie knew.

A distant howl from a restless coyote interrupted her chaotic thoughts. Glancing through the window, she watched the last rays from the setting sun glisten through the glass. Nightfall gently blanketed the lodge.

The butterflies knocked against each other as they resumed their frenzied dance. So much for staying calm, cool, and collected. Dixie was scared brainless and smart enough to admit it to herself.

No sense worrying about something she couldn't do anything about at the moment, Dixie stood. It was time to forage in the kitchen and see what she could come up with for a meal. Chicken salad sandwiches simply didn't sound like the right type of food to carry out a seduction.

Heck, who was she kidding? She no more knew how to seduce someone than she knew how to change oil. Only this, she couldn't pay her mechanic to help with, at least not legally.

The soft hiss of the lantern was a serene contrast to Dixie's chaotic thoughts as she rummaged for the chicken salad she was certain she'd put in the cooler. Ah, right under the bag of apples. It only took a few minutes to prepare the sandwiches and chips.

Glancing into the darkness outside the kitchen window, she wondered what was keeping Jack and the dogs? Maybe Dixie had scared him off with her forward behavior when they'd kissed. Dixie shook her head—her instincts had appeared to be on track judging by the way he'd responded.

Besides, if he'd hightailed it back to Denver, she'd win the lodge by default.

I don't want him to leave. Even if it meant the lodge was hers, at this moment, it was the man and not the contest that filled her with longing.

This was ridiculous—Jack hadn't left. His vehicle

was still outside and he wouldn't have kidnapped Sadie.

Barking echoed in the pines. Jack was home.

When had she started thinking of the lodge in so familiar a way? It wouldn't do to become attached, to the lodge or the man. Neither was a sure thing. When emotions were involved, nothing was a sure thing.

Panic welled within her, nonspecific, but real. Dixie had to slow down, remember who and what she was, and recall all the reasons she'd avoided romantic involvement.

The door from the kitchen porch swung open.

"You'd be amazed how far the lantern light shone from the window, we followed it back." Jack spoke softly, as though aware any loud noise or sudden move would startle her.

"Sandwiches du jour for dinner." Dixie avoided looking at Jack, pulled a chair out and sat. The dogs scrambled to the food bowls she'd filled earlier. It was time to get herself together and stop reacting to the man like a lovesick teenager. Time to reclaim her inner power as an independent career woman.

Jack claimed the chair across from her and picked up his sandwich. "I appreciate the meal."

Wham.

Dixie felt all of her bravado about independence and avoidance of involvement hit the proverbial wall. Just the sound of his voice set her off-kilter.

"Dixie?"

She must have been staring. What a dolt he probably thought her. "Hmm…sorry. Work stuff on my mind. No problem about the sandwiches, we have to eat."

Jack popped the tab on his soda and took a swallow before speaking. "I can understand about work stuff getting in the way. It can be difficult to keep it from taking over, crowding out everything else."

"Yes." Dixie rested her elbows on the tabletop and leaned forward. He understood. Although her words had been a cover for her wayward thoughts of him, they were true. "Sometimes I get so involved in my work, in what the kids need, or some problem they have I have trouble separating from it."

Jack finished chewing as he stared at her with a thoughtful look on his face. "Sometimes when I investigate a case and learn both sides of the situation, I want to get out of it."

"Why?"

Hesitating, Jack stared into the glow of the lantern. "Well, most often I'm investigating a spouse suspected of having an affair."

Dixie sat up and folded her hands in her lap. She'd never given much thought to what he did, to the details of his profession. "Why do you want to get out of the case sometimes?" She softly encouraged him to continue.

"When you look at it in black and white, it's wrong. If I find out the clients' suspicions are confirmed, that adultery is being conducted, it's a betrayal." Jack stopped speaking and seemed to gather his thoughts. "Then, I take a look at the spouse who hired me, the life they live, and all of the circumstances. It gets into shades of gray when I can understand why some of these people look outside their relationship for something that doesn't exist within it.''

''You condone extramarital affairs?'' She forced her tone to remain neutral so that he would not feel he couldn't continue.

''No, and that's where it all gets screwed up. I want to believe in happily ever after, but how do you do that when all you see is the other side?'' Jack stopped and took a bite of his sandwich as though embarrassed at having shared so much of himself.

The graveness of his tone told Dixie as much as his words. In some ways, at least in this way, they were more alike than he realized. Dixie wanted in her most secret heart of hearts to believe in the possibility of real love that lasts, but she'd watched her mother with four ex-husbands.

Waiting for Jack to finish his sandwich, Dixie's thoughts wandered in several directions. What type of relationship did his parents have? Did he believe in any type of love relationship?

With her fingertips, Dixie rubbed her temples where the beginning of a headache tapped incessantly against her optic nerves. Too many questions wanted answers in response to his sharing. And no way to ask them without sounding naive and ignorant. But, maybe Jack wouldn't judge her that way.

''Jack, how is your parents' relationship?'' she ventured.

"I don't remember. They died when I was five and my aunt raised me. With a little help from my uncle Vincent. Nothing like being raised by a spinster aunt and a bachelor uncle to give a guy no clue on a normal male-female relationship." He leaned his chair back and folded his hands behind his head.

"I'm sorry, I didn't realize..."

"No problem. How about you?" One eyebrow lifted. "Did your parents model 'happily ever after' for you?"

Dixie tried not to snort soda out her nose as she laughed softly in response to his words. "Sorry about that, I guess you'd have to know my mother to know why that's funny?" She mentally sorted through ways to describe Estelle to this man. To anyone wanting a brief description of her mother. It just wasn't possible.

"My parents divorced when I was less than six months old, I never knew my father. He is an international attorney and lives in Europe. Financial support is in his vocabulary, but not 'daddy.'" Dixie tried to keep her tone light to hide the long buried hurt. "Mother married three times after him, each time convinced it was forever. I have more junior bridesmaid's dresses in storage than most bridal boutiques carry in stock."

Jack placed his hands, palms down on the table and leaned forward. "I'm sorry."

If he'd tried to brush aside the story with platitudes or, worse, offered her a hug and a shoulder to cry on, she could have left it there. But the sincere feeling conveyed in his simple words brought a mist to her eyes. Furious at the show of weakness, Dixie blinked quickly before an actual tear could escape.

"Yeah, well, it all turned out okay. Mother is content, at the moment, to pursue her painting. She's realized it has been the one constant in her life." Pretending a nonchalance she was far from feeling, Dixie stood and tossed her paper plate and napkin in the trash.

Enough sharing, it made her feel vulnerable to him and that was the last thing she wanted. Wasn't it?

Jack watched Dixie pretend to clean the kitchen. He'd seen how their conversation had initially relaxed her and allowed her to open up. Then, as though a shade had come down, the camaraderie in her eyes had been replaced by caution. A skittishness. Like a snitch who decided it was too risky to spill at the last minute.

It was frustrating, but Jack knew to push now would only force her to close tighter. Why did this bother him? He barely knew the woman, and after the contest would likely never see her again.

The last part of that thought bothered him most.

What was so different about Dixie? He dated, met women in different places, socialized and traveled. So why was this woman so intriguing? Because she made him think, challenged him to explore the reasons behind his thoughts and beliefs, relaxed him even as she excited him, and made him smile.

Just like any other woman.

Yeah, just keep telling yourself that, Powers.

Her engagement had him stuck in a bad place.

He shook his head to clear the unwanted thoughts. "Oh, thanks for the fresh towels. I forgot to thank you when I found them this afternoon."

Dixie stopped repacking her cooler and looked at him with confusion on her face. "What towels?"

"The ones on the bed. Monogrammed, white towels."

"Do I look like room service? I haven't touched any towels but the one I used at the spring." She absently rubbed Sadie's head when the dog nudged her idle hand. "What type of monogramming?"

Jack straightened. Either she was pulling his leg or they'd had a visitor. "They match the pillowcases on my bed."

"The ones we found in the chest?" Dixie walked back to her chair and sat as she nibbled a ragged fingernail.

"I presume." He didn't like the worry he'd placed in her eyes by his questions. If he'd known she hadn't done it, Jack never would have brought it up. "Odds are I put them there this morning and forgot."

Or she was a good actress. Maybe she'd put them there after their shared kisses, and was now embarrassed by the show of softness toward him.

"You think?" A bit of the stress seemed to ease from her eyes.

Or was it relief that he was backing off on the questioning.

"I'm sure. Who else would be way up here? And

the two dogs would have noticed a stranger even if we didn't." *That's enough, Powers. You're overdoing the reassurance.*

"Then you don't think someone—"

"No."

Dixie's eyebrows rose at his quick reply. In his haste to put her at ease he was behaving out of character. Even someone who had only known him for a few days, as Dixie did, would sense that.

Jack stood. "Why don't I take the dogs out one more time before bed?"

"Thanks, I'd appreciate it."

"Hey." Jack tipped her chin up with a finger before he passed. "You made dinner. This is a partnership."

The smile that softened Dixie's lips made Jack wish they were not opponents. Made him want to know what might have been possible between them if they had met some other way. Some other time.

Tigger and Sadie raced ahead of him when Jack walked to the door. He glanced once more at the woman and caught a look of confusion in her eyes. Confusion about what, he didn't know.

Dixie waited for the door to close before releasing her breath. Thank heavens Jack had finally left the room, she seemed to have trouble remembering the basics of respiration when he was close.

Breathe in. Breathe out. That's a girl.

The spot he'd touched under her chin burned. Dixie probably had Jack's fingerprint branded onto her skin. *Breathe in. Breathe out. Use your brain cells, Dixie.*

Dixie needed to keep her wits about her or she'd never make it through the remaining hours, much less days.

Focus, Osborn, or tall, dark, and tempting will walk away with the lodge…or worse, your heart.

Damn, now she experienced brain drain even when he wasn't within touching distance. And what had Jack been talking about before he took off with the dogs? Something about towels?

His questioning at first had been adamant, but he'd let the subject go too easily when she'd shown a smidgen of apprehension. What did he expect? The thought that some psycho towel deliveryman was wandering around the lodge made her uncomfortable. What was it the kids always said about psycho serial killers movies? Oh, yeah—as long as one didn't run around in one's undergarments and smash against a window so the bad guy could see his next target, one was safe.

Somehow the advice didn't make Dixie feel any better.

Maybe Jack had simply forgotten and put them on the bed this morning. But he didn't seem the type to be absentminded. He seemed to be on the other extreme with his quick-witted questions and comebacks.

Or, worse than either possibility that had come to mind, maybe Jack was trying to scare her into leaving so that he would win the lodge. No, he wouldn't do that, would he? Some men might, but Dixie would bet her left thumb, Jack had integrity.

Hello, earth to Dixie. Does it really matter what the towel conversation was about?

Grasping the lantern handle, Dixie moved into the great room. The swinging light cast shadows, darkened already dark corners and basically scared the bejeebers out of her. Maggie would laugh herself into a coma, right after she wet her pants, at Dixie's fear.

Dixie marched up the stairs and into Jack's bedroom. She'd confront the mystery towels herself and see what was what. Stepping over the threshold, Dixie froze.

A crackling fire burned in the grate casting a yellow-orange glow over the bed. And the bed…the bed was exquisite.

It was turned down. Quilts and sheets perfectly folded over to offer an inviting picture. In the middle of the white quilt lay an enormous bouquet of wildflowers. Freshly picked. Not limp and aged.

This wasn't funny. Jack hadn't gone upstairs before he'd eaten dinner and she'd passed this doorway since the afternoon and it held a perfectly made bed, a cold, bare grate and definitely no flowers.

As she contemplated whether to run for the car or brandish the fireplace poker as a weapon, another idea popped into her frantic thought pattern. But it was worse than thinking a random psycho had popped upstairs to make the room as inviting as the most quaint bed and breakfast establishment.

Jack had done all of this. Climbed up to the win-

dow and done it before he came in for the sandwiches. No wonder he had taken so long. Of course,
it made perfect sense. He thought by scaring her he'd
win the lodge by default when she ran screaming
from the building and didn't stop until she reached
Pagosa Springs.

Ha. Jack didn't know he was dealing with a
woman made of sterner stuff than that. But Dixie
would feel much better when Sadie was back. A
wimp her dog might be, but she was a wimp with
large canine teeth.

Like Sadie would sink them into Jack. The dog
had lost her heart to the man within fifteen minutes
of meeting him.

Another thought hit her, maybe Jack hadn't
intended to scare her at all. Perhaps he'd designed
it to melt any remaining resistance, to set the perfect scene for seduction. And pure seduction it
was…inviting and tempting.

Turning back toward the door, something incongruous with either theory caught Dixie's eye.

The window.

She walked several steps back into the room. Her
stomach lurched. The latch was still upright. Locked
tight. From the inside. And as difficult as it had been
for Jack to open it from the inside yesterday, Dixie
couldn't imagine it being opened from the outside.

No way.

No how.

Oh, man.

Forcing a calm she was far from feeling, Dixie

turned toward the door. Her feet felt the urge to run, her mind wanted to take up flying by flapping her arms if necessary, and her heart just wanted it all to be a ridiculous mixup with a rational explanation.

Stopping short of the doorway, she laughed softly. That was it. A mixup. Yeah, the maid from the next abandoned lodge over had mistakenly prepared Jack's room rather than her boss's. Not even in a bad "B" movie would that theory wash.

It was time to confront the only other person who might have an answer. A logical, explainable solution.

Walking quickly she spun around the doorjamb and into the hall.

The man she collided with grunted in pain. "Is the house on fire?" Jack rubbed his chin where the top of her head had collided with it.

Thankful for bladder control muscles, Dixie punched Jack on the shoulder. "You scared me half to death. Why are you sneaking around? It isn't going to work you know." Breathlessness forced her to pause.

Jack rubbed his shoulder. "What in the world is wrong with you, woman? You could have heard us coming a mile away." He waved a hand toward the dogs sitting behind him. They were unusually subdued and watching her with heads tilted.

Like *she* was the nutcase here.

Great, now Jack and the dogs thought she'd lost it. "Well, how do you explain this?" Dixie stepped backward and pointed into the bedroom.

Jack stepped forward and looked. Rather than denying involvement, he immediately pulled her out of the room by the wrist. "Stay here. Lantern."

Dumbfounded, Dixie relinquished the lantern and watched as Jack strode to the window and checked the latch. "I already checked it. Locked from the inside." She resisted adding a sarcastic, "Duh" on to the end of the sentence.

She didn't like the frown marring Jack's face as he flipped back the sheets to look beneath them. The flowers scattered, some falling to the floor.

"Jack, tell me you're just trying to scare me. It's just your sophomoric way of trying to win the lodge." Her words begged him to admit involvement in some type of prank.

Instead of answering, Jack called the dogs into the room. He motioned Dixie inside, as well. "You're sure you didn't do this?"

Dixie shook her head.

Jack glanced back toward the bed again. "I'm going downstairs, stay here."

Although Dixie wanted to argue, to insist she wasn't helpless, she moved to the bed and sat on the edge. It wouldn't be fair to leave Sadie and Tigger alone just to go with Jack and prove a point about her level of personal courage. Besides he was the trained professional. Yeah, that was it, Jack was trained to snoop out suspicious activities, Dixie was trained to help kids. No contest. She'd wait.

After Jack disappeared through the door with the lantern, the light from the fireplace was the only illumination available. The dogs sat looking at her as if for some type of profound guidance.

Yeah, right.

"Oh, for heaven's sake. Lay down." She pointed at the rug in front of the fire. "I haven't lost my mind, just my common sense for entering this stupid contest to begin with."

After sniffing all corners of the room and even putting his head under the bed, Tigger moved to the rug and lay down. Sadie curled next to him.

The sound of footsteps on the stairs brought Dixie off the bed and reaching for the fireplace poker. Before she had it within her grasp, Jack entered the bedroom, balancing a rocking chair against his hip while trying to carry the lantern. She hurried to relieve him of the light.

Jack placed the chair next to the bed and motioned her back onto the bed. He settled into the chair, his face free of expression.

"Okay, out with it." Dixie sat cross-legged after climbing back onto the high bed. "What in the world is going on?"

Jack set the chair rocking and seemed to search her face before speaking. "I didn't do any of this to the room."

She looked straight into his eyes and the directness in their depths told her there was no doubt he was telling the truth.

"Neither did I." Dixie resisted the urge to scoot closer to the rocker.

"Some wood is missing from the stack out back

and two pieces were dropped on the ground." He anticipated her next question. "I notice details, it's what I do for a living. There were no logs on the ground this morning."

"Oh."

"Whoever did this—" he waved his arm to indicate the fire and bed "—knew the layout of the lodge. They knew where to find the towels, they knew how to move around the place without being detected. The question is why?"

"Maybe Mr. Granger arranged something." She grasped for a reasonable explanation.

"He would have informed us."

"A neighbor?"

Jack shook his head. "How many houses did you pass on your way here? I counted zero once we left the town limits."

"So we have an intruder who lights fires, turns down beds, and leaves flowers."

"Don't forget the towels." He grinned.

Dixie felt some of the tension leave her shoulders. "It does sound ridiculous. You're not worried?"

"Let's just say I'm cautious. The doors and windows are all locked, and we have the dogs." He watched the sleeping dogs.

Dixie smiled. "And hey, I could use a stick of wood as a weapon."

Should she feel apprehensive? Here Dixie was with a relative stranger, attractive though he was, miles from anywhere. Not to mention he wanted the same lodge she wanted.

How hard would it be for him to knock out the competition and simply say Dixie Osborn had never arrived at the lodge? No, that wouldn't cut it, her mother had spoken to the man.

Jack smiled and shook his head. "I don't want this place enough to get rid of anyone for it."

She was embarrassed he'd read her thoughts so easily. "How did you know?"

"Honey, your face is as easy to read as any I've come across."

Jack had called her "honey." So. Maybe he called all women honey. Maybe it was a derogatory term rather than an endearment.

Dixie stared into the fire to avoid making eye contact. She didn't want him reading her thoughts again. It was disconcerting. "So, what do we do?"

"The lodge is as secure as I can make it and I'm tired. We all stay in the same room and get some sleep."

Is he out of his mind? No way was she sleeping in this bed while he slept in the chair next to it.

"The bed is big enough for both of us." Jack unlaced his hiking boots.

For the love of pizza.

"No way...that is unacceptable...why don't you—"

"Move over." Jack stood and removed his boots and jacket. He stretched his arms above his head and rolled his neck. "I'm tired, you're tired, and we're adults. If you think you can't restrain yourself from touching me enough to share the bed, sleep in the rocker.''

Dixie's mouth dropped open. If *she* couldn't restrain *herself?* Who did he think he was? Brad Pitt? Hugh Grant?

Dixie folded both arms across her chest and lifted her chin. ''In your dreams.'' She would show him she wasn't some frigid, nervous spinster.

Jack turned the lantern mantle knob and extinguished its light. Dixie scrambled to the far side of the bed when he sat on the edge. Her pulse pounded in her ears. So much for pretending indifference.

Okay, this was no big deal. Sharing a space out of necessity. Two grown people in full control of their actions—if not their thoughts.

Dixie swallowed hard to keep from vomiting all over Jack's broad shoulders.

She could do this.

She would do this.

And there was no way Dixie would let him know it was the first time she'd slept with a man. In *any* manner. If she didn't know better, she'd swear this was something Maggie would rig just to put Dixie in this position.

If only it were that simple. The thought of a stranger wandering around the lodge, even if his or her actions so far were harmless was a bit disturbing. And to have to share a bed with the man whose kisses made her forget her name…well, that was pure sick torment from a higher power.

Mind over matter—mind over matter.

She jumped when Jack stretched out on his side of the bed and stared into the fire. Dixie would just pretend it was her mother next to her all night. That would solve the problem.

"Dixie?"

Her mother's voice had never sounded so deep and husky. Damn. "W...what?"

"Go to sleep. Stop that crazy imagination. I won't touch you."

Sputtering, she lay down and tried to relax. Her arm and hip lined up with the edge of the bed farthest from Jack. "I know that."

Full of himself wasn't he? As if she'd let him touch her. Or rub her back. Or kiss her neck just below the ear. Or any of the other two million things her crazy imagination was tormenting her with.

As if.

CHAPTER EIGHT

DIXIE snuggled back into the warm quilt. The horn blared again. Soft morning light warmed the log walls of the room. Flopping onto her side she sought the warmth offered by the body behind her.

A muscular arm snaked around her waist and pulled her against a muscled male chest. Her curves settled into his angles and Jack's breath warmed the back of her neck.

Jack. A man. In her bed. Touching her.

Shooting upright, Dixie smashed Jack's nose with the top of her head.

She scrambled to the far side of the bed.

"What in the name of—" Jack was sitting up with both hands cupping his nose.

"You touched me." Dixie tried to stop the squeak in her voice. "You said you wouldn't touch me."

Pulling a hand away from his face, Jack looked into his palm as though checking for blood. "You spent the whole night glued to me, I figured you were cold."

Sadie and Tigger peered at them from the edge of the bed. Two tails thumped the floor in unison.

A horn blared again.

Dixie and Jack jumped.

Jack leaped from the bed. Tigger was instantly at

his side. "Stay put," he told Dixie as he headed toward the door.

A car door slammed. Since the room was at the back of the lodge Dixie couldn't peek out a window.

"In the house." A female voice called from outside. "This is the Pagosa Springs police department responding to your request for an officer."

Suddenly Dixie looked down at her rumpled clothing. Then at the bed so recently and obviously shared by two people. The person outside might be a total stranger, but Dixie didn't want anyone thinking anything had happened, because it hadn't.

Dreams don't count, girlfriend.

Jack pulled his boots on, then opened the bedroom door. "Let's go down before she wakes the skunks. Come on Tigger, Sadie."

"Hey. Wait." Dixie scrambled to the edge of the bed. "Why are the police here?"

I knew it. Jack is a felon and they're here to drag him off to the pokey.

"I radioed them from my car when I was outside securing the lodge last night."

Sure you did.

Jack seemed to sense her skepticism. "I'm a private investigator, so my car is equipped with a citizen's band radio. I called down to report a suspicious occurrence, thought we might be able to learn more about this place and the man who built it." He cocked his head and smiled at her. "Satisfied?"

Dixie slipped off the bed and found her shoes, willing the heat in her face to subside. So much for a relaxing couple of days in the mountains. Time to face the new drama that seemed to be her life.

Jack walked down the steps behind the dogs and put a small smile on his face. No sense alarming the police officer when he opened the door by being a grump. Although she knew what he did for a living because of the radio call last night, it wouldn't do to irritate the local law.

Jack pulled the latch back and opened the front door. The dogs dashed around the small, dark-haired woman standing on the other side with her hand upraised, just stopping herself short of knocking on his nose.

What was it with women and his nose this morning?

He took note of the name on the uniform and offered his hand. ''Officer Church. Jack Powers—I made the report last night.''

Jack glanced at the police cruiser parked next to his truck. He noticed a man behind the wheel, but the dim early-morning light made identification impossible.

Why didn't the other officer come to the door with his partner?

Stepping around Jack, Dixie extended her hand. ''Good morning. I'm Dixie Osborn.''

''Pleasure, I'm sure.''

Jack noted a touch of sarcasm behind the seemingly innocuous greeting. What prompted that?

''Let me take some information to make the report

official and satisfy the chief.'' Officer Church flipped a small notebook open and looked questioningly at them.

Dixie glanced up at Jack with a look of puzzlement in her gaze, she'd obviously noted the other woman's curt tone.

"I'll need your names."

Jack swallowed his frustration, they'd given their names when he'd opened the door. "Jack Powers. P. O. W. E. R. S."

The woman stopped writing and looked up at him.

Good, she'd heard the sarcasm in *his* tone.

"Sir, this is not a matter to be taken lightly. It is an official filing of a police report."

Dixie looked back and forth between Jack and the police officer. "Jack, would you see about starting a pot of coffee so we can sit and relax while we talk to the police? Officer Church, maybe your partner would like to join us while we get the report filed."

Jack admired Dixie's tactful diffusing of a tense situation, a subtle starting over. Giving a nod, he headed for the kitchen. No sense antagonizing the local law.

Yet.

Dixie smiled at Officer Church, hoping the gesture would erase the worry lines forming on the woman's forehead, and repeated her earlier invitation, "Would your partner like to join us?"

"He's not my partner, at least not my police partner." The policewoman closed her notebook.

''That's Clyde, my husband. When we heard a report had been filed involving the lodge, I volunteered to do the call.''

''We appreciate it.'' Dixie tried to keep the questions from her eyes. Why would this particular call be of interest to this woman? And her husband.

Officer Church turned and motioned to the man waiting in the patrol car with a wave of her arm. The man shook his head.

''Clyde is a bit shy, excuse me.'' The woman stalked off toward the car.

Dixie listened to the comforting sounds coming from the kitchen, the clatter of a pan, a soft yip from one of the dogs, and a boisterous whistle. What was the song Jack was blasting with such enthusiasm? Unable to place it, she shrugged and watched the interaction between the officer and her reluctant spouse.

The motions seemed comical. The woman nodding her head and the man shaking his. Though Dixie was too far away to actually hear the words, in her mind she wrote the dialogue to match the motions.

Clyde, get out of that car now.

Ain't gonna do it, precious.

Then why'd you come out here?

Cuz.

A step sounded behind Dixie. ''Here's your coffee.'' Jack's voice broke her mental enactment of the scene she viewed. Heat swept across her face as though Jack could read her thoughts and knew what she'd been thinking.

Dixie nodded her thanks and accepted the cup. Heat seeped through the solid ceramic mug and warmed her hands. She lowered her face to hide her blush and sniffed the aroma steaming upward.

Ah, heaven on a cool, mountain morning.

Jack sipped from his cup and nodded toward the play unfolding next to the police car. "What seems to be the problem?"

"Seems Officer Church's husband rode along, but he's a bit of an introvert."

Jack shook his head. "For crying out loud—hold this."

Pushing his mug into her empty hand before Dixie could respond, Jack approached the couple with purpose in his stride.

Jack better watch it or Officer Church would cuff him and haul him straight to the local jail. She and Jack hadn't seemed to exactly hit it off.

Jack tempered his impatience. It wasn't as though he had a day of investigating and clients ahead—there was no need to be in a rush.

As he'd already met Officer Church, Jack focused on the unknown entity. "Morning, sir." He stuck his hand through the open window.

After only a second's hesitation, the man offered his hand for a handshake and nodded.

Sensing a bit of man-to-man interaction might be appreciated, Jack turned to the officer. "Ma'am, the coffee is ready. How about…" He paused and turned back toward the man.

"C...C...lyde Church." The formerly silent man offered his name.

Jack faced the officer again. "How about Clyde and I take the dogs for a quick walk then we'll come inside and complete that report."

Officer Church seemed to teeter between maintaining a position of control with her husband and the need for caffeine.

Caffeine won.

"That seems like a good idea." Still unsmiling, she joined Dixie on the porch and the two women walked inside.

Jack turned his attention to the car's occupant.

The man opened the door and stepped out. "Good morning. I like the way you handled Imogene. One in a million, my woman, but a bit of a tough nut to crack."

Jack couldn't believe it, the shy man who had seemed to stutter only moments before, was a raving talker. Must like his wife to think otherwise.

"We appreciate you and Officer Church coming so far out to look into this situation."

"Oh, no problem. It's what family does."

"Family?" Jack matched the man's pace as he approached the dogs who'd dashed down the porch steps toward them.

Clyde Church blushed. "Well, Imogene doesn't much like folks knowing our link to the lodge, though the better part of three counties already does. No keepin' a secret in a mountain town this small. The poor woman was determined to come and I couldn't very well let her drive into the wilds on her own.''

Jack sighed, seemed every question was going to take ten minutes to discern the kernel of an answer. ''And family figures into this equation, how?''

Smiling, Clyde glanced toward where Tigger and Sadie wrestled for control of a stick before running into the trees together. ''Well, sir, my great-uncle built this lodge. So, when there is any type of commotion that involves it…we try to help out. You know…family.''

Running a hand down his face, Jack winced when he encountered his still tender nose from Dixie's collision with it earlier. Had that really been only this morning, within the past hour? It seemed more like weeks ago.

''Are you telling me things happen here often?'' Jack motioned toward the lodge.

''I wouldn't really say often, but with April 26 coming up this week, we half expected something.''

Clyde scratched the back of his ear, reminding Jack of a slow-moving basset hound. Quick response was obviously not the man's forte.

Patience. Aunt Emma would be proud of Jack taking time to remain calm rather than yanking the words from Clyde through his nostrils.

''Why is April 26 significant?'' Jack asked.

Jack could almost hear the gears in Clyde's head as he tried to form a sentence and decide what to say.

Finally glancing around as though making certain

they were alone, Clyde leaned forward. "Now, I'm no expert on a lot of things, but the lodge I know about."

"Yes?" Jack prompted.

"Well, we really don't like to talk about it outside of the family."

Dixie approached from the lodge. Clyde stopped, glancing quickly about as though to see that his wife was nowhere near.

Dixie looked at Jack with her eyebrows raised. "Um, Officer Church is having a look around the lodge. Did I interrupt anything?"

"Clyde is sharing a bit of history on the lodge." Jack stated. He looked at Clyde. "Dixie can be trusted."

Clyde hesitated a moment more, then sighed as though unable to resist sharing a bit of gossip, even with his wife close by. "Since Cynthia jilted Uncle Bill at the altar, we've all tried to forget. But the more eccentric he became the more we remembered."

Warming to the idea of an audience, Clyde motioned them closer to him in a secretive manner.

Jack smiled. The man was milking his fifteen minutes of fame for all they were worth. He didn't blame the man and wanted to hear more. At least now he had a good idea what the letter C on the embroidered linens stood for...Cynthia.

"Well, we should have known there would be trouble. Cynthia never did anything in a normal or understated way. She met Uncle Bill at a dance in the spring, oh, I'd say it's been twenty years ago now." He paused dramatically and took a breath.

Jack would bet his left ear the man knew how long it had been down to the minute and seconds.

"Poor Bill never stood a chance. He was poor, but a hard worker. Came into town each weekend from his place, though he hadn't built the lodge then." Clyde shook his head. "Cynthia had been away for a couple of years of college in Denver and fancied herself quite the cosmopolitan. Dressed differently than most folks in these parts, and the makeup. Lord have mercy. You could see her lips coming an hour before the rest of her arrived."

Chuckles erupted from Clyde, as he seemed to be remembering the sight. Jack waited patiently for the man to continue and Dixie drummed the nails of one hand on her opposite forearm.

Dixie tried to still her fingers. But it was impossible. Once they started their dance of impatience there was no stopping until the urge passed. She wanted to hurry the man along, learn more about the lodge. But she knew the man was enjoying the limelight, so Dixie put on her proverbial listening cap and waited. Impatiently, it was true, but she waited.

After a couple of long guffaws, Clyde drew a deep breath and leaned forward. "Now, where was I? Oh, the lips. Not normal red or pink, she wore orange lipstick. Always. Orange. Anyway, that really doesn't have anything to do with the story. It just makes me laugh to remember the sight."

Jack straightened. "When did your uncle Bill decide to build the lodge?"

"Well, after about four or five months of daily courting, Bill gathered up every bit of his nerve and proposed to Cynthia. And for some reason the girl said yes." Clyde stopped. He shook his head. "Not that Bill wasn't a decent sort, but the two of them together simply didn't make sense. They wanted such different things. The minute she said yes, Bill put himself in hock up to the top of the hair follicles on his head and started building a home, as he put it, worthy of his Cynthia."

Dixie forgot to drum her fingers as she felt the devotion and love poor Bill must have felt for the flighty Cynthia. All of his dreams focused in one place, his future, and his heart. Part of her wanted to stop Clyde, to keep the rest of the story silent as though that could change the outcome.

"The man built most of the place by hand, picked everything about it himself. Like facing the master bedroom window toward the east so that the morning sun would wake his Cynthia each morning." Clyde paused dramatically.

Dixie saw Jack start to move toward Clyde as though to help him through the story. Obviously he wanted the ending to come sooner rather than later. Didn't Jack see what was coming? Didn't he care?

Clyde seemed to sense Jack's impatience as well, and perhaps afraid of losing his captive audience, he continued in a rush. "He even hand-carved the wedding bed they were to share. For months he worked on nothing else but this place. During the entire process, Cynthia insisted she wanted to wait until it was finished before she set foot inside it.''

"Oh, but how could she stand not to be a part of it?'' Dixie wondered aloud. How could a woman not want to be part of the process of creating her future home?

Clyde nodded. "My thoughts exactly. A woman's home is personal. She should have had some kind of interest in it. That lack of interest should have been Uncle Bill's first clue something wasn't right. But he was so smitten, nothing punctured his happiness.''

Jack smiled at the man. "I'm sorry to interrupt, Clyde, but how did Bill end up losing the lodge?''

"That's the worst part of the story. On the day of their wedding, everybody in the town showed up. It was a big affair, per Cynthia's request.'' Brushing imaginary lint from his sleeve, Clyde paused and looked them each in the eye, one then the other, to gain maximum dramatic effect. "Three o'clock rolled around, the time they were to wed. Then three-fifteen. Three-thirty. By four, most of the guests had gone home. But Bill refused to leave. He stayed at the front of the church. Finally Cynthia's mother went home and returned with a note she'd found on her daughter's bed.''

Dixie's heart jumped. "What did it say?''

She didn't want him to continue, but couldn't stand for him not to…as though watching a train wreck in slow motion knowing there was no way to prevent the devastation and destruction to come.

"The note had two lines. Ten short words. Ten words that changed Bill Peterson forever." Clyde stopped, took a deep breath before continuing. *"Want to live in the city. Marrying Timothy Bart. C.* Bill never said a word. Timothy Bart was the president of the bank where Bill had borrowed the money to build the lodge, a childhood rival since primary school. Cynthia and Timothy left for Denver that day and never looked back."

Dixie sniffed, but refused to cry outright. "And then your uncle closed the lodge?"

"Closed is a polite way to put it." Clyde shook his head. "He walked out of the church that day without saying a word, and no one's heard him say one word since. He made his payments to the bank as best he could, but never bothered with the taxes. So, the government finally took the place to cover the back taxes. Occasionally old Bill wanders into town. Some say he lives in a cave nowadays."

That poor, poor man.

She could imagine the devastation he'd felt. The shame, the feeling that it was better to live alone than risk himself or his heart ever again. So many of the teens Dixie worked with came to her with the same thoughts running though their minds and hearts. Rejected, so often, by the very people who were supposed to love them best. They turned their back rather than taking the chance of being hurt again.

But, then, didn't she do the same thing? Why had she always avoided romantic relationships? Why did

Dixie feel any relationship she became involved in was doomed to failure?

Dixie knew the answer. She'd watched her mother try again and again and again, to find soul love, real love. Each time Dixie watched as it crumbled. Who was to say the same thing wouldn't happen to her? Why risk the devastation?

Glancing at Jack, Dixie caught him rolling his eyes. He was as bad as some of her hormone-impaired teenagers at the center. Trying to act like the sentimental story hadn't touched him.

"Clyde!" Officer Church's voice rang from inside the lodge. "Get in here and help me look around."

Bolting like an electrocuted rabbit, Clyde nodded at Jack and Dixie, then loped toward the lodge.

"Well, looks like his reflexes are okay." Jack laughed. "At least in response to his wife's yell."

Dixie stared at the doorway Clyde had disappeared through long seconds after he was no longer visible. Finally she turned back toward Jack.

"We have to help him," she stated.

"Help who? Clyde?" Jack shook his head. "He's well and truly stuck with his wife."

"Not Clyde. The uncle. Bill." Dixie glanced around at the trees ringing the clearing, half expecting the reclusive man to be watching or listening.

Jack crouched and brushed pine needles into a pile with his long fingers. "What do you mean help him?"

"I don't know how to explain it exactly." Dixie needed him to understand why they should help the man who'd built the lodge she and Jack were competing to win. "Find him. Make sure he has a decent place to live. Help find a way to pay the back taxes."

Jack stood and looked down at her. "You're serious aren't you?"

Dixie swallowed hesitantly. *"Yeaaahhh.* Why not?"

"Because we don't know him." He held up a finger. "Because we don't know how much of that story is true." Jack held up a second finger. "Because you can't save the world." A third finger came up.

"Why not?"

"You're serious." Jack shook his head. "Are you some kind of crusader?"

"No, yes, well...not exactly." Dixie angled her chin upward, refusing to be embarrassed. "I just like to think I can make a difference."

Jack whistled. Sadie and Tigger straggled out of the nearby pines, panting and playing. They ran toward the steps and collapsed together on the ground near Jack's feet.

Jack rubbed the top of Tigger's head, earning a lopsided grin from the pup. "How do you plan to make a difference?"

Dixie twirled a length of her hair between her fingers and stared off into the trees. "I guess it's difficult to put into words so much stuff...about the kids I work with, their hopes, their frustrations, their fears...I want to believe I can make a difference in their lives and in the lives of the people they will touch someday. Uncle Bill's situation feels the same way to me, someone who has been hurt and has lost their trust in the world and people.''

Was Jack really listening, understanding, or even paying attention? Dixie felt like an idiot for the impassioned speech she'd made in reply to his question.

"How old are the kids you work with?" Jack questioned.

"Teenagers, mostly. Teenagers without direction, most of them without real families." Dixie motioned toward the lodge. "Can't you imagine the benefit time here would give, counselors to talk to the kids, learning survival skills to build their self-confidence, team building experiences?"

"Can't they get those benefits somewhere in the city?" Jack continued. "The lodge is pretty remote."

Dixie smiled and looked around. "Exactly. That's why it's perfect."

Dixie's words rang in Jack's head. He could picture the concept she was trying to relate. And he agreed with it. Teens would enjoy the type of experiences she envisioned. God knew it would have kept him out of some trouble when he'd been that age.

Dixie didn't realize she'd just shared her dream for the lodge. Jack liked that she was so comfortable with him that it had slipped out unnoticed and naturally. Her dream was a noble one.

But Emma would love the lodge, too. It's why she'd secretly entered his name in the contest. Jack had to remember his responsibilities to her. All of the years she had sacrificed for him, Emma deserved the peace living at the lodge would bring. The security it would give her.

Jack hated that in order to fulfill Emma's dream it would mean killing Dixie's.

Damn.

Neither spoke. Each seemingly lost in thought. Jack didn't share why he wanted the lodge, it seemed like the wrong time…the wrong way. As though to pipe in after Dixie opened her dreams to him would belittle them.

"Mr. Powers?" Officer Church and her husband came onto the porch, breaking the silence.

Jack walked toward her, "Yes, ma'am."

"We've done a walk-through of the property, and a perimeter check." Officer Church flipped her notebook open. "I have both of your names and contact information, the report will be filed as soon as I get into town."

The notebook snapped shut.

Jack hoped his face didn't show his skepticism. Nothing the officer had done was new to what he'd already accomplished, other than filing an official report.

"We appreciate you driving out." Jack offered his hand to Officer Church and then her husband. "Clyde, thank you for your time."

The man's explanation on the history of the lodge had been informative and helpful, if it were true.

"N…n…no problem." Clyde's stutter was back in full force with his wife present.

Dixie stepped forward. "Is there anything you recommend, Officer Church?"

The other woman looked at Jack before answering Dixie. "Yeah. Lock your door."

Jack resisted shaking his head. The officer hadn't said the doors, but "door"…her meaning clear. She obviously didn't approve of the reason the two of them were in the lodge…alone. Tough.

As the patrol car turned and headed away from the lodge, Jack glanced at Dixie. Her small shoulders were shaking…was she crying about poor ol' Uncle Bill?

Then, laughter erupted from between her lips.

Dixie held her mirth as long as possible, at least waiting until the squad car was out of hearing. Then she released the laughter building inside. Aware that Jack was looking at her as though she'd lost her mind, Dixie tried to reign in her glee.

Holding her hands to the muscles in her sides, then wiping the tears from her eyes, she turned to Jack. "I swear we have to be on a hidden camera or something."

Jack stared at her for another couple of seconds, before allowing his lips to tip upward, then he shook his head. "It does seem a little more than weird."

"Like one of those ridiculous reality shows…tune in to see what it takes to drive our two contestants nuts…the strange, hermit man of the woods or the actors we hired to play Officer Church and her eager to share the details husband." Dixie giggled. "I'm glad you were here to witness everything, too. My friends will never believe any of this. I may need you to back me up once we return to Denver.''

Jack watched her for a moment, then narrowed his eyes. ''Did you just ask me out? Aren't you engaged?'' he teased.

''I, well, not exactly. What I meant was—'' Dixie stopped verbally floundering when she saw the smile that replaced the smoldering glance. The dweeb had been teasing her. She was thankful not to have spoken the truth…that seeing him again was something Dixie definitely wanted. Possible womanizer or not, his smile and tempting kisses had her off balance and wanting more.

A horn sounded in the distance, from the direction the police car had taken. Another horn beeped.

''What in the world is that about?'' Jack stepped off the porch and walked toward the road.

Dixie tried to put some energy into wondering the same thing, but found herself much too interested in watching the broad-shouldered man's walk.

Pure temptation in flannel and denim.

Dixie was in trouble.

A car drove into the clearing, too fast for the condition of the road. It wasn't the patrol car returning, but a large black sedan.

Now, Dixie was curious. Who the devil was wandering all the way up to the lodge? It wasn't time for the coin toss, so who would be going out of their way to find the place…especially in a fancy car better suited to city driving.

"Jack?" Dixie called out, trying to figure out who was approaching.

The man shrugged and stood waiting for the car to pull up even.

Slowing, the car rolled to a stop behind Jack's truck. There were two people in the car. The driver and a passenger. As the passenger window unrolled, Dixie stared. It wasn't possible. Please, Lord, anything but this.

A hand wearing several rings and bracelets waved at them through the open passenger window.

Dixie looked back and forth between the approaching nightmare and Jack. This could not be happening.

"Yoo-hoo, Dixie. I'm here, darling." The woman attached to the arm called out.

Oh, yeah, it's happening.

Dixie watched with the fascination of someone seeing a multicar pile-up...horrified, but unable to look away from the carnage to come.

Estelle Osborn had arrived. What in the world had Dixie done to deserve her mother showing up at the lodge?

Jack listened to the high-pitched, shrill voice. It was somehow familiar, but he couldn't place it.

The cell phone.

The call he'd taken for Dixie.

Her mother's voice on the line.

What in the world was the woman doing in the wilds of the Colorado Mountains? Had Dixie known she was coming? Was it some kind of plot to get him to give up the lodge?

Judging by the horror and shock on Dixie's expressive face, this was an unexpected surprise.

Turning back toward the car, Jack watched the woman open her door, then lean back in to say something to the driver.

Who was crazy enough to drive the woman up the pothole-ridden road to the lodge?

A man opened the driver's door and stood.

Uncle Vincent?

Was this family reunion day? There coming toward Jack was his uncle. And on his arm was, evidently, Dixie's mother.

There had to be a hidden camera somewhere. Jack barely resisted the urge to shout to the hidden microphones that he knew what was going on and the game was up.

Unfortunately Jack somehow knew it was just plain bad luck, and not Hollywood, that had two people that should have been in the bustling city of Denver…walking toward he and Dixie at the lodge. In the middle of nowhere.

The woman released Vincent's arm, and held out both arms to Dixie. "Honey, Jack's uncle and I almost never found this place."

Dixie grimaced as she accepted her mother's hug. "Mother, what in the world *are* you doing here?"

"Bringing you breakfast, now where is that nice man I spoke with on the phone?" Estelle looked toward where Jack faced the other man. "You know, the one who is brave enough to teach you to cook."

Dixie turned to look at Jack, who stood glaring at his approaching uncle.

Jack shook his head. "Uncle Vincent."

The other man grabbed Jack's hand for a firm handshake, while patting his free hand on Jack's shoulder. "I know what you're thinking, Jack. But between Emma and Estelle there, I didn't stand a chance."

Dixie wondered at the power Emma obviously had in Jack's life to send Uncle Vincent checking up on her opponent.

Jack pulled Uncle Vincent away from Dixie and her mother. "Don't get me wrong, it's always great to see you...but what are you doing here? How did you find the place?"

"Seems your competition's mother was worried, tracked you down through Emma, Emma called me, I returned Estelle's call...and here I am." Vincent looked a bit dazed. "Actually it's been a blur. The next thing I knew I was volunteering to drive her so that she wouldn't try to find the place on her own."

"Well, let's go meet this dynamo who got you behind the wheel." Jack turned and headed toward where the two women talked softly. "Dixie, I'd like you to meet my uncle, Vincent Powers."

Dixie stepped forward and shook the older man's hand. "A pleasure. And Jack, I'd like you to meet my mother, Estelle."

Jack tipped his head and shook the lady's hand, "Ma'am."

Estelle laughed. "We're not strangers. After talking with you on the phone, I feel like I've met you already. Call me Estelle."

"Yes, ma'am…I mean Estelle." Jack looked at his uncle. "My uncle tells me you are one persuasive lady."

"Well, once I started thinking about my Dixie up here in the mountains, with heaven only knows what kind of maniac…" Estelle gave Jack an apologetic look. "That was before I knew you, of course. I decided to make certain everything was all right."

Dixie looked frozen in place. Jack had not seen her speechless before, and it seemed uncharacteristic.

Dixie gave herself a mental shake, the reality of her mother being at the lodge finally sinking in. Not to mention, Jack's uncle. It seemed like a bad joke, and if she didn't know better Dixie would think Maggie had a hand in the fiasco.

No, swapping nightgowns was one thing, sending her mother to the lodge, another.

"Did you say something about breakfast?" Dixie tried to keep her mother focused. She had to find a way to get her mother alone for a moment to fill her in on her false engagement to poor Guy.

"Oh, I nearly forgot." Releasing Dixie's arm, Estelle turned to Vincent. "Would you be a dear, Vinnie, and grab the groceries from the car while Dixie shows me around this…place."

Dixie saw Jack shake his head as his uncle headed toward the car and Estelle took Dixie's arm and led her inside.

"So, tell me all about the lodge." Estelle stopped inside the front door and looked around. "Well, it's certainly big."

Knowing her mother as she did, Dixie heard the words unspoken…dirty, remote, hopeless…all of the things Dixie refused to see in the place. All she could see were the possibilities.

Leading her mother inside, Dixie started whispering the details of her "engagement" and begging her mother to not reveal the untruth to Jack.

Jack followed his uncle to the car and helped him unload several grocery bags. Together, they carried them inside and placed them on the kitchen table.

Suddenly the lodge, which had felt large and wide-open, now seemed overcrowded with the two uninvited guests. Jack didn't even try to figure out why it rankled him to have his time alone with Dixie threatened. All he knew was that he didn't like it.

At all. When had Jack and Dixie lost control of the situation?

The scents coming from the bags drew Jack's attention back to the things he could control. "What did you bring?"

"Estelle couldn't decide what sounded best and she didn't know what you might like." Vincent pulled item after item from the bags, each wrapped in foil. "So, we have biscuits and gravy, pancakes, sausage and bacon, scones, French toast, oatmeal and fruit. I don't think we'll starve.''

Jack helped open the packages. He heard Dixie coming back down the stairs with her mother. Estelle's excited voice carried, but he couldn't distinguish the words. Until they came into the kitchen.

''Baby, you're twenty-seven. If you want to have physical relations—who am I to judge? You are old enough to make that decision.'' Estelle patted Vincent's arm as she took a paper cup filled with coffee from him. ''I mean, look at Jack, for goodness' sake. If you hadn't wanted to enjoy each other I would be more worried.''

''Mother.'' Dixie's gaze darted from Jack to Vincent to the ceiling. What in the world was her mother up to? Dixie had filled her in on her ''engagement'' to Guy upstairs. She mouthed the numbers, one through ten. ''Jack and I are not involved, physically or otherwise. I've told you that.''

''So you are simply enjoying an affair behind poor Guy's back?'' Estelle did not seem disturbed by the thought.

Jack decided to take mercy on Dixie. After her explanation of her mother last night, and the short time he'd been exposed to Estelle, he knew drastic action was necessary.

''Ma'am, I guarantee, tempting as your daughter is, we did nothing Guy might question.''

Dixie stiffened next to him. ''What? Jack, I'm a grown woman. I can speak for myself.'' Dixie blew the bangs from her eyes. "Mother, nothing happened. We are both trying to win this lodge. Nothing more."

"What a shame, dear." Estelle sighed. "Jack so reminds me of Paul, my second…no third, husband."

Stamping her foot, Dixie looked ready to blow.

Putting his lips on Dixie's seemed the only reasonable way to stop the words that seemed ready to erupt. Jack didn't expect the jolt the contact brought. After a moment's hesitation, Dixie relaxed into the kiss.

Though he had a feeling he'd pay for it later.

He was sure of it.

Dixie swallowed her words when Jack's mouth came down on her lips. The kiss rocked her even more than his protecting of her reputation in front of his uncle and her mother. For heaven's sake, didn't anyone realize she wasn't a child who had to explain every thought or action.

She stiffened for only a moment before her body convinced her brain this was good for both of them, her mind and libido.

Jack cupped the back of her head with his hand, threading his fingers into her hair. She felt weightlessness settle into her legs. Respiration again went the way of Lala land.

As Dixie's lungs reached the point of bursting from the breathlessness caused by the gentle pressure on her lips, Estelle cleared her throat. Loudly. Indelicately.

Jack's hands settled on Dixie's shoulders as he took a step back. She was thankful for the support, and had the feeling he'd known she would need it. His expression was unreadable and his lips compressed. Had the kiss affected him at all?

Vincent grabbed Jack's hand and shook it enthusiastically. "That's it, my boy. Decisive action has always been the Powers way."

Vincent grabbed the roll of paper towels and thrust them into Estelle's hands. Dixie wasn't sure whether to laugh like a moron or start blubbering like a baby. What in the world was going on? And could Dixie extricate them from the mess without hurting sweet Uncle Vincent and her drama queen mother? Jack might have thought he was saving the day by being old-fashioned and chivalrous, but he'd only managed to make her want to push him into the spring.

And just what did her mother mean by, *what a shame.* Dixie wasn't a pariah for heaven's sake, simply picky about men. And she'd just told her mother of Dixie's false engagement to Guy. What in the world was Estelle doing?

Suddenly Dixie's thoughts focused. The route was clear. She'd strangle Jack in front of the two witnesses and the contest would be void. Simple. The lodge would go to the center and *her* kids. Except Dixie wasn't certain if he'd stand still long enough for her to pull a chair over to stand on. Dixie wanted a good straight shot for maximum wringing ability.

Of course, then she'd have to deal with her fake engagement to Guy—was she too old to just run away?

Jack stepped to the far side of the table as though aware of the direction of Dixie's earlier murderous thoughts. "I know Dixie is more than able to speak for herself, but I felt I should be the one to explain. I know she is engaged to Guy, and I respect that."

Patting her mother on the shoulder, Dixie jerked her head toward the back door as she met Jack's gaze.

It was time for a talk.

Now.

"Why don't we round up the dogs while your mother and Vincent explore the lodge. Give them a chance to absorb the news." Jack seemed to understand her message. He moved toward her, grasped her elbow and pulled her toward the back door. "If you'll excuse us."

Estelle's spoke. "All right, but I want to be in on the planning of your wedding to Guy, Dixie. Maybe an autumn wedd…"

Her voice faded as Jack dragged Dixie onto the back porch.

She twisted her arm free as the door clicked shut. "Okay, Einstein. What in the world was that fiasco inside?"

Vincent and Estelle appeared at the kitchen window peering at them curiously.

"Oh for Pete's sake." Jack grasped her hand in his larger one and headed into the trees.

Dixie jogged to keep up with his ground-eating stride. "Hey…could we…slow down?"

"Sorry." He stopped and released her hand. "Is your mother always so interested in everything?"

She rested her fists on her hips. "No more than your uncle." Jack had some nerve insinuating her mother was a busybody. So what if she was, it wasn't his business to judge. Not with his uncle's nose pressed against the same window as her mother's.

Jack rubbed his hand down his face. "Okay, let's see if we can reroute this comedy of errors before things get worse."

"So not only is my mom a snoop, but now being stuck in a bed with me all night is the worst thing you can imagine? Don't tell me you're worried about word getting out." Irrational she may be, but for crying out loud, they'd just slept in the same bed pressed close together, and kissed—she was way out of her comfort zone.

Jack took a step toward her. "Dixie, get a grip."

His expression should have told her to tread carefully, but she ignored the not so subtle body language Jack exhibited. "Just because you are used to sneaking around and spying on people doesn't mean everyone else—"

Reaching across the narrow trail Jack pulled Dixie against his chest, his hands gripping her upper arms. The breath whooshed from between her lips a millisecond before he kissed her into silence.

For the second time that morning.

Dixie's arms slipped from his light grasp easily

and she wrapped them about his neck, straining closer. What started as a spontaneous move by Jack to halt angry words became an aching encounter.

Only the light brushing of Jack's tongue across her lower lip brought sanity rushing back. Dixie dropped her hands to her side and stepped back without meeting the man's gaze.

What in the world was wrong with her? She couldn't control her limbs or lips when Jack touched her. She didn't want to, only wanted to feel more, to move closer, to experience an ache Dixie had merely dreamt existed.

"Okay, no more kissing. I'll stay perfectly rational." Dixie finally looked into his face. "Why in the world did you feel the need to defend us as though we were teenagers and they'd caught us fooling around?"

"Look, your mother had just seen a bed we obviously shared. I didn't want her getting hysterical or anything."

"My mother has had four husbands. I don't think it would have shocked her." It more likely thrilled her to death to think her daughter had done something so completely out of character. "This is not the Victorian era. People actually know about reality."

Jack paced up the path, and then back again. "I understand that. Call me old-fashioned but I didn't want to show disrespect toward your mother. And when news gets back to your fiancé, I wanted you to have a ready defense."

Dixie stared at his back as he paced away again.

Well, chivalry seemed to be alive and well in one Jack Powers. What a refreshing change. Her respect for him grew even more.

Not that any of it really mattered. Dixie had to keep focused. The center. The kids. The engagement to Guy.

"Tell you what. We only have a couple more days to get through. It won't do much harm to coexist in front of everyone." Dixie tucked her hands into the back pockets of her jeans. "We'll have our coin toss, then move forward with our lives. Separately."

Jack stopped and looked at her for long seconds before he answered. "Agreed. Besides, your mother and my uncle will probably be gone by nightfall so it'll only be one day of acting. I think we can handle that."

Dixie hoped he was right. Somehow, it all seemed too easy. Nothing that seemed easy ever stayed that way. Maybe just this once it could be the exception.

All she had to do was not think about the taste and feel of Jack's lips on hers.

Yeah, right.

Jack listened to Estelle. And listened. And listened. He and Dixie had returned to the lodge to find his uncle and Dixie's mother waiting.

Dixie had braved the combined front and taken the subject in hand. Grasping Jack's hand, she held up her other hand to stem questions. "Mom, Mr. Powers, Jack and I would like you to relax and enjoy your time with us." Estelle moved toward them.

"Mother." Dixie stopped her mother's movements by shaking her head. "We can discuss my wedding plans when I get back to Denver."

Vincent subtly took Estelle's elbow and steered her toward the table. "Let's eat something before my nephew collapses from starvation. We Powers men have large appetites."

Estelle efficiently set the table. "Jack, would you be a dear and fetch the rocker I saw upstairs."

Jack willingly complied as it gave him a chance to escape the scrutiny downstairs and refocus his thoughts.

Stepping into the bedroom he looked at the scene as Estelle and Vincent might see it. Rumpled bed, wildflowers strewn on the bedspread and the floor, and the fire a glowing bed of coals.

Oh, yeah, a scene set for seduction if he'd ever seen one. It didn't matter that the time he'd spent with Dixie in the bed had been totally innocent. Well, mostly innocent.

What had gone on in his mind and dreams didn't count as reality.

It had been pure torture having Dixie's warmth seeking his through the night. Jack had resisted all of the ungentlemanly urges her nearness had brought to mind.

Walking to the window, he watched Sadie and Tigger playing.

Nothing sexual had taken place between he and Dixie last night and, yet, he'd never felt so good in bed as he had during those long hours of listening to her soft breathing. How was it possible?

What *were* the dogs doing? Their roughhousing pulled him from his thoughts. They seemed to be playing tug-o-war with something. It wasn't an animal or a stick.

Jack turned from the window, picked up the rocker and headed downstairs.

Laughter and the murmur of voices came from the kitchen and he carried the chair to its place at the table. Dixie's face glowed with a blush—she playfully punched his uncle on the arm.

She was beautiful. And off-limits since she was engaged to some man named Guy. Jack had an objective. So did Dixie. They simply happened to be opposing goals. They each wanted, no, needed, the same thing.

The lodge.

"Vincent, can I see you before we sit down?" Jack wanted to take a closer look at what the dogs had found and fill his uncle in on the strange happenings at the lodge.

"Certainly, my boy. Ladies, if you will excuse us." Bowing slightly from the waist, he turned and followed Jack out the back door.

Stepping outside, Jack closed the door behind the other man. "I want to check the dogs."

The men approached the playful pair and Jack whistled. Sadie turned immediately and Tigger followed with a length of cloth clenched between his teeth.

Jack dropped down and rested on his heels. He held his hand toward Tigger. "Give." The dog dropped the "toy" into his master's hand.

Vincent moved closer. "What's that?"

Jack inspected the cloth, which turned out to be a man's flannel shirt. In good shape, dirty only where the dogs had dragged it through the leaves. It wasn't his and the lodge was miles from the nearest neighbor. It seemed their mysterious visitor had met the dogs this morning, but how had the dogs gotten the man's shirt?

Turning to his patiently waiting uncle, Jack stood and handed him the shirt. "Someone has sneaked into the lodge at least once since Dixie and I have been here."

"Was anything stolen?" Vincent inspected the sleeves.

"No, it was just weird stuff. The bed turned down, fresh flowers left, towels moved to a different location." He sighed realizing as he spoke how ridiculous it sounded. "Nothing harmful. But I'm concerned someone is out here and keeps coming inside. What if he walks in while Dixie is alone?"

"Does she know about it? Are you sure it wasn't Dixie?"

"Yes, she knows about it, that's why we shared a room last night. And unless she's a hell of an actress, Dixie is as puzzled about it all as I am." Jack tossed a stick for Tigger. "That's why you saw the patrol car leaving, we filed a report."

"Just how long have you and Dixie known each other?"

"About a week, since the drawing for the contest." He patted Tigger's head when the dog leaned into his leg.

"Short time to know someone." Vincent smiled. "Swept you off your feet, has she?"

Jack blinked at his uncle's pinpointing of something Jack didn't even want to acknowledge himself. "Something like that."

Vincent turned his attention to the shirt again. "Well, there are no tears in the sleeves or on the bottom edges, and no bloodstains so we can presume the dogs didn't forcefully remove it from the person."

"It also means they didn't bring it far or it would be dirtier or torn. He was nearby when you arrived." Jack scanned the tree line. It was unlikely the person was still there, but he scanned the area out of instinct. "Your arrival probably scared him off."

"You think we need to report it to anyone besides the sheriff in Pagosa Springs?" Vincent carefully folded the shirt while the dogs looked at it longingly.

"What would we tell everyone? Someone's been treating us like guests, delivering flowers and wears good quality clothing?" Jack gave a quick snort. "I saw the reaction from the deputy who came out this morning. They don't seem to feel it's anything serious. Some kind of local situation."

"Well, then I'll simply be an extra set of eyes and ears for you while we're here." Vincent glanced toward the house. "But I don't want Estelle alarmed, how 'bout we keep this quiet?"

Raising his eyebrows, Jack grinned. "You sound a bit protective. How long have you known Dixie's mother?"

"Almost as long as you've known her daughter, nosy." With those words, Vincent headed back. "I don't know about you but I'm starving."

Jack shook his head and followed. He'd never seen his uncle this interested in a woman. The dry cleaning store had been his passion for as long as Jack could remember. As much as investigating could wear him down, Jack knew if he'd gone into the family business he wouldn't have survived six months before he was running through the streets of Denver screaming from sheer boredom.

Ah, well. People chose their own destiny. To some extent. Fate did have a way of throwing well-laid plans out the window.

Dixie looked up as Jack and Uncle Vincent entered the lodge. "We thought you fellows decided to use the hot spring or something. That or our ghost spirited you away."

Estelle gasped. "Dixie, we don't ever joke when speaking of those in the other dimension."

Jack tried to catch Dixie's eye, but she wasn't paying attention.

"Oh, Mother. Unless ghosts are able to turn down beds and pick flowers, I don't think we have anything to worry about. Our intruder is flesh and blood."

''Pack your suitcase.'' Estelle stood, tipping her chair to the floor. ''We're leaving.''

Dixie smiled. ''Mom, I'm twenty-seven years old. Not to mention if I leave I forfeit the lodge.''

''And I'm fifty...'' Estelle glanced toward Vincent. ''Well, Dixie, I'm your mother. Living in the sticks is one thing, fighting off a mysterious criminal is another.''

Jack cleared his throat. ''Estelle, trust me, if I believed Dixie were in danger, I'd carry her to town over my shoulder if necessary.''

Dixie slowly turned to face Jack, surprise appeared in her eyes for a moment and then the look disappeared. He wasn't even certain it had been there at all.

Reluctantly turning from the soft light that remained in Dixie's eyes, he continued. ''Let's eat and we'll head into Pagosa Springs. There wasn't anything in the rules about taking time away from the lodge to relax.''

Everyone sat around the table and chose from the smorgasbord of choices available.

Jack chewed his biscuit and wondered what had gotten into him. If he played his cards right, Estelle would convince Dixie to go back to Denver and he'd win the lodge for Emma by default.

Jack watched his uncle blush again when Dixie touched his arm and laughed at something the man had said. What was it about Dixie that made those around her smile more often?

Or maybe it was just Jack who noticed the way

she moved, her natural spunk and intelligence, her—
okay, this was ridiculous. He was here with an objective, to win the lodge, not to romance an engaged
woman. No matter how tempting. Yeah, so why did
the lodge keep slipping from his mind while the
woman was easing more often into his thoughts?

Not to mention his fantasies.

CHAPTER NINE

SOMETIME later, they rattled down the pothole-ridden track in the rental car Vincent and Estelle had driven. Jack gripped the wheel with both hands to keep control of the vehicle on the rough surface of the primitive road.

How in the devil had his uncle managed to make it to the lodge? But, he supposed if Dixie could make it in her heap this car had probably done fine.

Sadie and Tigger hadn't seemed to mind being left to guard the lodge. But maybe they didn't realize they were on the job. The dogs probably thought it was time to play while the humans were away.

Jack glanced at Dixie seated next to him. Estelle had insisted the two of them share the front seat of the sedan while she and Uncle Vincent sat in the back.

Swerving to avoid another large rock in the roadway, Jack grinned. He'd learned in the first fifty feet of driving that the slightest sideways motion of the vehicle caused Dixie to lean into him. Each time their shoulders brushed together, a blush colored her face.

He liked it.

A lot.

''So, my boy, think we should do some research

on the former owner of the lodge you mentioned while we're in town?'' Vincent broke the silence.

Jack caught Estelle's wide-eyed look in the rear-view. The color had drained from her face. Where had Dixie learned her spunk when her mother seemed so timid about everything?

"It wouldn't hurt." He chuckled. "But I'm not sure what the local law enforcement will think of an intruder who does nothing but 'kill' his victims with kindness. They weren't overly concerned this morning."

Dixie rolled her window halfway down. "You almost have to feel sorry for the man. *If* it's him."

Estelle crossed her arms. "It's repulsive. Sneaking into someone's home and touching their things. People like that need professional help."

"Mom, the poor man was left at the altar. The woman he loved walked away from him and the life they'd planned." Dixie half turned in her seat to face her mother. "*If* it's him, and that's still a big if, I feel sorry for him. To love so deeply, one might never get over it. To lose a dream." She faced her window and closed her eyes as the breeze washed over her.

Jack forced himself to watch the road rather than the woman. He couldn't believe he was actually jealous of the small strands of hair brushing her cheeks. From the time he and Dixie had spent snuggled together under the quilt through the night, he knew just how her skin felt...and smelled.

Fresh and clean. Inviting and warm. But, forbidden. And definitely not in his plans.

The remainder of the trip passed in silence. None of them seemed inclined to offer an opinion on the mystery visitor after Dixie's impassioned defense of the former owner of the Crazy Creek Lodge.

Jack mulled her words in his head. Reading between the lines, he heard the yearning for her dream reflected in her tone. Although seemingly realistic and logical on the surface, Dixie harbored a soft heart. A dreamer's heart.

How did she manage to keep such an iron grip on her optimism? Working with at-risk and runaway teens she had to have been exposed to the darker side of life. And, yet, she still appeared to have a Pollyanna disposition that was real, not affected, like other women he'd come across in the dating world.

"Did you see that sign, Jack?"

Dixie's fingers on his arm brought him back to the situation at hand. He wondered how many times she'd tried to get his attention. Judging by the delicate furrows between her brows, enough times she probably thought he'd been ignoring her.

No, just thinking too damned much about her.

"I'm sorry. Working through a case in my head." Jack asked silent forgiveness for the untruth. "Afraid I must have missed the sign. Anything important?"

Dixie seemed to realize her hand still rested against his forearm and pulled it away. Jack missed its warmth.

"Just a sign for Pagosa Springs, its only five more miles."

The road surface finally changed to pavement. Unfortunately, it meant no more accidental bumps on the shoulder from Dixie.

I'm turning into a wimp. When a mere brush of contact from a female caused his nerve endings to kick into overdrive he was on the verge of pitiful. Or the woman was a stick of walking, talking dynamite.

Jack would lay money it was the latter reason.

Dixie watched through the windshield as the town of Pagosa Springs came into view. She'd only spent a small amount of time in it when she'd arrived, and that had been after dark.

Set amongst rolling hills dotted with ponderosa pines, it was a picturesque sight. A lake to the right glittered with the light from the sun that had topped the mountains to the east. The contrast of light from the water and the shadowed greens of the scattered stands of trees made her smile. It was perfect.

Peaceful. Real. Clean. And still only a dream. What if it remained a dream after the coin toss? What would happen to her kids? Well, not actually hers. She may not have carried them in her body, but she certainly carried each of them in her heart. And no matter the outcome of the toss, she'd find a way to take care of the kids in her care.

"Dixie?"

Estelle broke the silence and startled Dixie from her thoughts.

"Yes?" The serenity of the scene was momentarily shattered by reality.

"We saw a sign for the hot springs when we passed through town, do you suppose they are sanitary?"

Vincent coughed to cover a laugh.

Dixie smiled and half turned to look backward. It was good to know some things never changed. Her mother's aversion to anything common was one of those constants. "I'm sure if it's a public facility monitored by the health department it will be fine."

Estelle patted Vincent's hand. "What do you think, Vinnie? Should we trip the light fantastic and try one of the springs?"

"That sounds like a fine idea." Vincent placed his hand over Dixie's mother's and left it there. "What do you think, Jack? You could show us some of those fancy dives that put you through college."

Dixie looked at Jack. "You were a swimmer?"

Jack signaled and turned onto the main street that ran through town. "I went through college on a swim team scholarship."

She tried to keep her gaze from traveling over his form.

"I know—I'm not what some would consider the 'typical' swimmer type. But it paid tuition."

"Um, I'm not one to be picky, but..." Estelle started.

Dixie looked straight ahead so her mother

wouldn't see the smile she couldn't suppress. If there was something Estelle was it was picky. But somehow, it never seemed obnoxious. Dixie's mother had a way of presenting things so that you felt it was your idea in the first place.

"What's wrong, Mom?"

"Dear, we didn't bring swimsuits."

Jack glanced at Dixie, warming her skin with his gaze. "I don't see a problem with dropping you and Uncle Vincent to do some shopping while Dixie and I do some investigating."

Estelle beamed. "Wonderful."

A few minutes later, after dropping Vincent and Estelle in the heart of Main Street, Jack pulled into the parking lot of the visitor center. He quickly turned the key, stepped out, then circled around to open Dixie's door.

She stared up at him in surprise. "Oh, thank you."

Jack wondered if anyone had ever opened a door for the lady before.

They went inside and looked at the wall of brochures on local attractions. A detailed map of the city covered one wall of the room.

"Howdy. Can I help you?" A short, white-haired woman had been kneeling behind the counter and now stood.

Jack and Dixie turned to face the woman.

He moved to the counter. "We wanted to do some shopping, then hit the hot springs pool."

"Are you staying in town long?" The helpful
woman smiled up at him.

Jack read her nametag. "Only a few days, Betsy.
We're staying out at the Crazy Creek Lodge."

Betsy's eyes widened and her lips formed a circle.
"Well, that's interesting."

Dixie joined them at the counter. "Hi. Maybe you
could tell us where we could go to do a bit of research on the lodge. It's an intriguing place and we'd
love to learn more."

Jack could almost hear the gears in Betsy's head
as she tried to form a sentence and decide what to
say to them first.

She finally glanced about the room as though making certain they were alone then leaned forward.
"Now I'm no expert on a lot of things, you might
want to talk with Clyde Church, Bill is his uncle."

"Yes, we talked with Clyde this morning," Jack
prompted. He'd like another viewpoint on the lodge,
other than a relative of the original owner. "We
hoped you might offer a different viewpoint, or more
information."

"Well, we really don't like to talk about it in my
family."

Dixie looked at Jack with her eyebrows raised.
Another relative…what were the odds?

Betsy sighed. "Cynthia is my cousin."

Warming to the idea of an audience, Betsy motioned them toward an informal sitting area. A
leather couch and several comfortable looking chairs
formed a half circle in front of a stone fireplace.

Although April, there was a fire crackling to take the chill from the air.

Once they had chosen chairs, Betsy stood and faced them with her back to the fire.

"Basically Cynthia was fickle as a magpie, and broke poor Bill's heart." She paused dramatically for breath.

Jack would bet his left ear the woman never tired of retelling the story, it was Pagosa's own personal soap opera.

Betsy seated herself on the hearth. "Cynthia had been away and when she returned to town, Bill fell for her the first time he saw her at a spring dance. He'd always been painfully shy around girls, but he actually got up the nerve to ask Cynthia to dance."

Chuckles erupted from Betsy, as she must be remembering the sight. Dixie drummed her nails on the arm of the chair. Jack leaned forward, resting his elbows on his knees.

Dixie laced her fingers together and rested her hands in her lap to quiet the evidence of her restlessness.

After a couple of long guffaws, Betsy drew a deep breath and leaned forward. "Where was I? Oh, the dance. Cynthia towered over Bill, they were awkward together, but he stared at her all night with total devotion. He was smitten."

A clearing of a throat behind them attracted their attention. Dixie turned to see her mother and Vincent standing nearby, each carrying a shopping bag.

How long had they been standing there?

Dixie saw Vincent give her mother his handker-chief. Estelle gently dabbed the corners of her eyes. Her mother's heart was as soft as her own.

Jack smiled at the woman. "I'm sorry to interrupt, Betsy, but how did Bill end up losing the place?"

"Well, I'm sure you heard that she left him, lit-erally, at the altar." Betsy saw their nods. "After that Bill kept to himself, did occasional odd-jobs and tried to keep up with paying off the lodge, but even-tually it was too much and the state took possession for back taxes that weren't paid."

Dixie shook her head. "And then?"

"And then, nothing. Bill wanders into town oc-casionally, but most don't hear him talk much."

Dixie was saddened, as she'd been when Clyde had shared the story that morning. As the sound of the final sentence faded, she sank deeper into her chair lost in thought.

Jack stood and offered his hand to Dixie to help her out of the chair. She stared at the hand with its sprinkling of hair on the back, its strength, and its tenderness. Taking a deep breath, Dixie placed her hand in his and allowed him to help her up.

When she was upright and free of his touch, Dixie risked speaking. "Thank you."

Jack grunted a reply and followed Betsy to the counter. "We appreciate you taking time to share with us, Betsy. You wouldn't happen to know where we could find Bill, do you? We'd like to meet the man who built the lodge."

"Heavens, no. Bill lives like a hermit. Never know where you might run into him."

The bell above the entrance rang as a family wandered into the visitor center. Betsy hurried toward the newcomers.

Vincent and Estelle joined Dixie.

Estelle rubbed her arms as though chilled. "How terribly sad." She looked up at Jack. "You think this is the person who has been sneaking into the lodge? You aren't going to hurt him are you?"

"Mom, for goodness' sake, Jack isn't going to hurt anyone." *Especially me, because I won't let my heart feel more for him than it already does.* Dixie turned to Jack. "Well, this is your area of expertise, what next?"

"Next, we enjoy our day and go swimming. The man hasn't hurt anything, no sense hunting him like a fugitive."

Dixie wasn't surprised by Jack's answer, only thankful. This was a side to the tough private eye she wouldn't have expected, but liked. Seemed his hard as steel exterior housed a kind, caring inside. She hadn't wanted to see it. Seeing it, Dixie would have had to admit how much the Crazy Creek Lodge might be a dream for Jack, as well as herself.

And that made it more difficult to be selfish, to want it for herself.

How could Dixie change the lodge into a place where dreams came true rather than a place where dreams had been shattered?

There was only one answer. But it was too hard to contemplate, much less act on.

Estelle watched Dixie and Jack. She watched them talk. The way they stood. The way their gazes followed the other when they thought no one watched.

After observing them all morning, Estelle had finally formed a hypothesis. They were absolute idiots when it came to the ways of love. Each did not possess the wisdom concerning love God had given to the least of his creatures. Even the lowly earthworm seemed to know more about love and courtship than these two.

No wonder Dixie had invented a false engagement to Guy. She was attracted to Jack and that scared her.

How could Estelle help them admit the attraction they had for each other?

CHAPTER TEN

DIXIE glared into the locker room mirror at her reflection one more time. How in the world had her mother managed to pull this off?

The suit she had trusted her mother to pick up while Dixie and Jack had been at the visitor center was not exactly what she'd had in mind,

When would Dixie learn to just say no?

Estelle had found them, what her mother deemed, *the perfect suits*. Dixie trusted that her mother had chosen something decent.

Trust, my eye. If Estelle hadn't been the woman who'd given birth to her, Dixie might have wished the plague or worse on her.

The suit her dear, sweet mother had chosen was not decent. It really could not even be called a suit, more like butt floss with a price tag. Okay, maybe it was more coverage than a thong, but not much.

How was she supposed to walk around in front of Jack with this on? The heat between them was already at the spontaneous combustion stage, this wasn't going to reduce the attraction.

"Mother, when you unlock the door to your bathroom stall, I am going to kill you." Dixie tried to pull the bottom of the suit down to cover more of, well, her bottom. But that simply left more of her belly naked. Flat it might be, but she preferred less skin visible.

"Now, Dixie, I simply chose something I knew would look lovely on you." Estelle placated her from the perceived safety of the stall. "You always cover your nice figure with such prudish clothing. We Osborn women have always been known for our hourglass shapes. It's time you showed yours to full advantage."

"This is not the time or the place." Dixie wasn't certain any place was right for the bright yellow bikini. The boost it gave her bust line was obscene, though the color of the suit did make it look as though her skin was flawless.

No, she would not fall into a fashion trap. Dixie just wasn't one to be flashy or call attention to herself with her clothing, of lack thereof. Maybe she could swim with her shirt on. Picking up the oversize college sweatshirt, she decided that would draw even more attention. Dixie would simply have to brazen it through and try not to be obvious she was uncomfortable in the suit.

"Between you with this scrap of material that calls itself a swimsuit and the sexy nightgown Maggie packed, I'm not sure which of you should be punished first." Dixie mumbled to herself and stopped looking for ways to make the bikini cover more as she waited outside her mother's stall. "You can't hide forever, let's see your suit."

Estelle inched the door open. "You'll be honest and tell me if I look ridiculous? I don't have the figure I used to and don't want to look like something I'm not.''

She stepped in front of Dixie.

"Wow." Dixie could think of no more perfect word. The red one-piece was daring, but tasteful. It was exactly what she would have chosen for her mother. "It looks like you. Flashy and classy."

Estelle did a little spin. "Do you think Vinnie will like it?"

"Are you sweet on him? Mother, you just met him." Dixie could tell by the gleam in her mother's eye she was interested in the man. "What makes him so special?"

"Oh, honey. When you know someone has that something extra, you just know." Estelle moved in front of the mirror and preened. "He is a gentleman, opens my door, is considerate of me, encourages me to talk and share and then he really listens when I do. Vinnie is different than most men. He's real.''

Dixie had to remind herself that her mother was talking about Vincent. Her description could have been Jack. A gentleman, good listener, considerate, and a dreamy kisser.

But still her rival.

Still the obstacle to a dream.

As she was to him.

Not to mention the woman in his life—Emma.

Just Dixie's luck to finally find a man to send her hormones into overdrive and he had to be her competition. And now her mother was sweet on the man's uncle. Could it get any more complicated?

* * *

Jack draped a towel over his shoulder and followed
his uncle out of the locker room. He glanced around
the pool area. Dixie and her mother were nowhere in
sight.

Just then he caught sight of Dixie. Or was it?

The woman looked like Dixie, though he'd never
imagined she would look like this in a swimsuit.
Even in his most vivid fantasies.

Jack stepped back into the shadow of the building
and watched Estelle and Dixie meet up with Vincent.
He could tell by the way Dixie let her long hair fall
forward she was self-conscious.

About what?

He watched as she retrieved a towel from the
nearby stack, wrapped it under her arms and tuck it
into place. It wasn't that cold. Could she actually be
embarrassed to stand there in the knockout bikini?
Surely with a body like hers she'd worn tiny bikinis
before.

Then, from what he'd learned about her so far,
maybe not. Dixie was certainly a study in contrasts.
From pure vixen when she kissed, to virginal minx
in a bikini designed to send a man's blood pressure
soaring.

Vincent turned and pointed in his direction. Estelle
waved and motioned him over. Time to face temptation in a lemon sherbet bikini up close.

"Estelle was just telling me about the shop where
she found the suits, my boy." Vincent stood next to
Estelle with a proprietary hand on her shoulder.

"By the looks of it, she picked the right suits." Jack smiled at Dixie.

Dixie met his gaze and raised her chin. Nervous or not, Jack knew she'd make the best of it. That was just the kind of woman she seemed to be, gutsy and proud.

Estelle and Uncle Vincent strolled to the shallow end and sat on the edge to dangle their legs in the steaming water.

"Should we ease in slowly or dive?" Jack teased.

Dixie's eyes widened momentarily, then she smiled and dropped her towel. "I'm going to dive. Let's see if you can keep up."

With that, she jogged the few steps to the edge and executed a clean dive.

A woman who knows how to swim. I like that.

Even more, he liked a woman who could issue a challenge and then have the guts to follow up on it. That he liked a lot.

Tossing his towel on top of Dixie's discarded one, he plunged into the pool and searched for the water nymph in the yellow bikini.

Laughter erupted again as Vincent demonstrated his latest movie star impression. Humphrey Bogart could well have been in the car with them.

But Dixie would no more have noticed the thick-browed actor than the man on the moon, her inner thoughts were still focused on the man next to her. The man who'd pursued and challenged her at the pool until she'd been breathless.

They'd taken turns terrorizing her mother and Vincent, slipping up next to them from under the murky, steamy water. Estelle would pretend to squeal, Vincent would pretend to save her and be rewarded a kiss on the cheek.

It had been easy for Dixie to see why Jack had made the swim team at the collegiate level. The man might well have been born with fins and gills. He was beautiful to watch as he swam or dove. The fact that he had the body of a Greek god didn't hurt, either. Hey, she was human.

"Oh, Dixie, do your Dolly Parton imitation, honey," Estelle urged. "Where she sings 'Jolene.'"

Dixie saw Jack's gaze flash down to her chest for a split second before he turned his attention back to the road. Her mother couldn't have picked Shirley Temple or someone else more innocent and under-developed.

She wasn't about to ruin everyone's fun just because her belly was flip-flopping from the hormonal surge Jack's attention provoked.

By extending the words and throwing in just the right amount of twang, Dolly Parton's voice seemed to spill from Dixie's lips.

Applause sounded from the other passengers when the last note faded.

Vincent patted her shoulder. "Encore, encore. How about one more?"

Dixie blushed. "Not unless you or Jack does a mean Kenny Rogers and we make it a duet."

Jack stopped the car in front of the lodge. "Not for any amount of money."

When Dixie moved to push her door open, Jack's hand on her other arm stopped her.

"Wait." Jack said.

Dixie waited. So did Vincent and her mother.

Jack's gaze darted from one end of the lodge to the other. He even swiveled in his seat to look behind them. *Now* he was making her nervous.

"Jack, what's going on?"

Jack stopped searching and looked at her. "Notice anything odd when we pulled up?"

"Of course not, we just—oh, the dogs." Dixie looked around. "They should have come running."

Estelle leaned forward. "Maybe they just ran off and didn't hear us."

Jack frowned. "It's a possibility, but I know Tigger. When I'm away he goes into guard mode. When anyone drives up or approaches, he comes running. I trained him like that for Emma's protection."

Dixie did a mental double-take. He lived with Emma?

Vincent opened his door. "Ladies, if you'll give us a couple of minutes we'll have a look inside the lodge and secure the perimeter."

Looking at his uncle, Jack grinned a lopsided smile. "Too many police shows."

"Hey, it sounded professional." Vincent smiled and stepped out of the car. "Are we going to chat all day or what?"

"Lock the car doors, Dixie. I'm sure everything is fine." Jack walked toward the lodge with his uncle.

No sooner had they disappeared inside the front door than Dixie's brain clicked into gear. This was not some gothic novel from the seventies, she was not helpless, and she was far from stupid.

She unrolled her window. "Mother, I'm going to have a look around."

"Baby, they told us to stay in the car," Estelle argued.

"And your point is?"

"Well, I suppose I don't have one. You have always been known for being headstrong." Estelle unlocked her door. "Let's go help those poor defenseless—*ahhhh!*"

Dixie started when her mother squealed, ramming the top of her head against the door frame. What in the world was her mother thinking?

Looking out the windshield as Dixie rubbed her head, she saw what had startled her mother. An older looking man stood in front of the car. His shoulders were slumped. The flannel shirt he wore was clean and bright, his face clean-shaven. His hair neatly combed.

Dixie felt her mother's hand on her shoulder, the nails biting into her skin through the fabric of her shirt. Dixie wanted to reassure her mother, but what could she say?

The man moved slowly toward the door, toward her open window. What had she been thinking to unroll it and unlock her door? Why hadn't Dixie listened to Jack? Why did she always have to be a crusader without common sense?

Then she noticed the flowers. A large bouquet of bright wildflowers in the man's right hand.

She raised her gaze to meet his. In his faded blue eyes she saw an echo of what he must see in hers, apprehension, caution, and... *Hope.*

Dixie opened her door.

Estelle squeaked from the backseat again. "Dixie, what are you doing?" she said.

At Estelle's words the man stopped. His gaze filled with fear and he looked toward the woods. Dixie could almost smell his desire to escape warring with the need to reach out to someone.

"Mom, I'm going to step out and greet our guest." Dixie said softly. "It's okay."

For once in Estelle's life she actually listened and was silent. Dixie stepped out of the car and faced the man. He was only a couple of inches taller than she, his age wasn't as old as she'd first thought. The posture and creased face making him appear older than he probably was.

"Good morning." Dixie kept her tone soft so he wouldn't follow the instinct written on his face and run away.

An inner battle seemed to wage in the man. Finally he seemed to make a decision. "For you." He offered the flowers to Dixie. His voice was raspy and soft as though seldom used.

Raising her arm she accepted the gift. "They're lovely. Did you bring the others?"

"Yes."

"They were beautiful, too." She took an appreciative smell of the flowers. "I'm Dixie."

"I know." He backed up a step.

"Please...don't go." Dixie resisted the urge to touch his arm to keep him from leaving and smiled. "You're Bill, aren't you?"

His eyes widened.

If she didn't do something he was going to run. "I'm so glad to finally meet you. Your lodge is beautiful. Your talent shows."

"Not mine anymore." The pain of this fact came through in his whispered words.

What could she say to that? It was the truth. "No, but with all of the work and caring you put into it, part of it will always be yours. Dreams don't just go away."

"What will you do with it if you win?" Bill appeared to know about the radio contest.

How could Dixie put all of her hopes and dreams into a few words that would explain it?

Only two were needed.

"Help children."

A smile slowly lit his face, brightening even his eyes. "I wanted there to be a lot of children here. That would be good."

"But, Jack might win. His plans would be good, too." Dixie defended the man in his absence without knowing what he might do with the lodge.

Bill seemed to consider this a moment. "Only one can win."

"I know."

Bill stepped closer and looked into her eyes. "What happens is meant to be." He touched the back of one of her hands and walked away.

Slowly, without rushing.

Dixie wanted him to stay, to answer all of the questions in her mind. Wanted to tell him that although his dream of a life with Cynthia hadn't come to fruition, there were other dreams that could become reality.

But he was already gone. Bill had disappeared into the trees, leaving only the flowers and a sad smile on Dixie's face.

Jack waited until the man vanished into the trees to come from behind his truck. When he'd watched from a window in the lodge as the man approached the car, his heart had pounded. Instead of following his first instincts and dashing out to keep the man away from Dixie he'd slipped out the back and moved close enough to help if necessary. And close enough to hear.

He'd heard Dixie defend his dream as much as her own, and she didn't even know what it was. Jack moved behind Dixie and gently touched her shoulder. She turned to look at him as two tears quietly slid down her cheeks.

"Did you see him, Jack?" Dixie nodded toward the spot where Bill had slipped into the trees. "What a gentle soul."

"I know. It's why I didn't interfere." He pulled

her against his chest and rested his chin atop Dixie's
head. "You have a lot of grit."

"Thank you for trusting me to handle it."

Estelle approached as Vincent came from the
lodge.

Jack stared into the trees where the man had disappeared. A life wasted because of a dream unful-
filled. A gentle soul like Dixie's hurt. How could
he prevent the same thing from happening to her?

Jack pulled Dixie closer. He didn't know how, but
somehow he would make sure her dreams became a
reality.

Following a light snack and small talk, Dixie convinced her mother that staying in town was better
than all of them staying at the lodge with its meager
furnishings.

Watching her mother driving away with Jack's uncle, Dixie tried to suppress the little voice in her heart
that whispered this was the final night before the coin
toss. That maybe that was why she'd been so determined to have the place back to the way it had
been…just she and Jack…and the dogs.

Whatever the reason, they were alone, and Dixie
felt suddenly awkward in the silence left by the de-
parting car. Birds still chirped, a breeze stirred the
aspen and pine, but Dixie could still hear the pounding of her heart above all of it.

Jack tossed a stick for each of the dogs, seemingly
oblivious to any tension…or excitement…swirling

between them. Was it only her imagination? Did Jack feel any of the attraction Dixie felt?

At that moment, Jack turned from the dogs and caught Dixie staring at him before she had time to turn away or conceal whatever might be written on her face.

The gaze he focused on her told Dixie more than she'd known seconds before. Jack wanted her. She might not know anything else he was feeling, but Dixie would stake her life on the mutual heat.

Breaking eye contact, Dixie cleared her throat. "I think I'll take advantage of the downtime and soak in the hot spring."

Jack tossed another stick. "Keep your eyes open. Maybe put your clothes on the bushes this time."

Grinning, Dixie entered the lodge. She'd have to keep an eye out for the baby skunk who'd been around her first time in the spring...and thank it.

Jack waited until Dixie whistled for Sadie and walked into the trees headed for the hot spring. Then, he dropped and started doing push-ups.

Deep and fast, twenty...thirty...forty...until he reached a count of eighty and collapsed onto the grass. The exertion had done its job and taken his mind off of thoughts of Dixie.

For the time it had taken to do the exercises. Now he was definitely wandering toward Dixie again with his thoughts.

What the hell was he supposed to do? She was engaged to another man.

Somehow, the woman had worked her way around his defenses. Jack wanted to stay focused on his goals, without a thought about how any of them would affect anyone but he and Emma.

But he couldn't.

Not anymore.

Dixie, without even trying, had taken first his breath…now possibly more.

He was thankful Uncle Vincent hadn't done anything but nod and agree when Jack asked him to stay overnight in town. Jack had wanted this time with Dixie. But, now that he had it, Jack wasn't certain.

He was always certain.

Always knew what he wanted and how to achieve it.

Except now.

He knew what he wanted, Jack simply wasn't sure he could have it.

And for the first time with a woman…it mattered.

It mattered a hell of a lot.

But how to convince Dixie to take a chance on him. Walk away from the other man in her life. Trust Jack. Because as much as Jack wanted Dixie physically, he wanted her trust more.

Much more.

CHAPTER ELEVEN

DIXIE soaked in the water. Floated and tried to relax, take herself somewhere within her mind where there was no life altering decision to make.

Where there was only sunshine and warmth. But that wasn't reality and she knew it. Plus, Dixie loved the occasional cloudy, drizzly day. It helped make the warm, sunny ones even more wondrous.

How had she managed to avoid heart damage till now? It had never been difficult before to lose herself in her work or some other cause. To just walk away when a man wanted too much from her.

This time it was Dixie who wanted more. She wasn't sure how much more, and wouldn't let her thoughts drift in that direction.

All she would allow herself to admit was that she liked Jack. Respected him. Even with the specter of Emma hanging between them, Dixie liked what she'd learned about this man.

The way he'd stayed back and trusted her to deal with the elusive Bill earlier. The manners he exhibited by always being a gentleman…chivalry with an edge. That was a good way to put it.

And, she had to be honest, the physical attraction was like none she'd ever experienced. Dixie pondered this as she slipped beneath the surface to wet her hair.

There were a lot of handsome men. Why this one? Why Jack?

Because her heart said so...not her mind. If it were only in her mind Dixie could dismiss it, could walk away...but with her heart making its attraction clear, she didn't know how to turn her back.

Dixie didn't want to.

Dusk was descending gently as Dixie made her way back to the lodge. Sadie ran ahead, probably eager to find Tigger.

Sniffing appreciatively, Dixie saw lantern light shining through the lodge windows. No, it wasn't her imagination, she smelled steak grilling.

Stepping into the kitchen through the back door, Dixie followed Sadie into the great room. There, Jack crouched in front of the fireplace. Tigger barked and ran in a circle around Sadie.

They were home.

"Where did you find that?" Dixie nodded toward the four-legged iron grilling rack perched over a bed of coals in the monstrous fireplace. On the rack were two steaks and two foil-wrapped objects.

"Inside the oven in the kitchen." Jack turned the steaks with a long set of metal tongs. "Hungry?"

For more than you know.

"Yes, is there anything I can help with?" Dixie draped her damp towel over the nearby rocker.

"Emma packed a bottle of wine if you would like

a glass.'' Jack waved toward the kitchen. ''It's open on the counter.''

Dixie wandered into the other room to pour a glass of merlot she found. Why would this Emma pack a bottle of wine when she knew Jack would be alone at the lodge with another woman? Did she trust his devotion to their relationship that much?

Taking the initiative, Dixie poured a glass for Jack. It was time to be blunt. Time to ask the questions that had her confused.

With only one night left before she and Jack went their separate ways, Dixie decided to be simply what she was…forthright and honest.

What did she have to lose?

Stepping into the great room with the two glasses, Dixie stopped…stunned. Jack had made use of the time she'd been out of the room and spread a quilt from the upstairs bed on the floor in front of the fire.

On it were plates heaped with steak and what must have been the contents of the foil packets, steaming potatoes and carrots.

''I had no idea you were a gourmet chef.'' Dixie struggled to appear calm and unflustered, glancing about for distraction. ''Where are the dogs?''

''I put them upstairs in my room.'' Jack watched her.

Her trembling hand revealed her disquiet as she handed him the glass of merlot she'd poured for him. Dixie quickly sat in front of the nearest plate.

''Hey, I was a Boy Scout, meat and potatoes are

my specialty." Jack laughed. "And about the only thing Emma trusts me to prepare."

Dixie grabbed the opening. "Emma sounds pretty involved in your life." *Oh, God, that sounded whiny and obvious.*

But, if it was, Jack didn't seem to notice. "Every nook and cranny."

Well, that was about a thimbleful of information.

Jack raised his glass and stemmed any more questions for the moment.

"To a worthy adversary. Not to mention a lovely one."

Dixie hesitated only a split second, wishing that somehow they had met as something other than competitors.

"Hear, hear." Touching her glass gently to the rim of his, she echoed his sentiments.

Several minutes passed as they enjoyed the succulent steaks and vegetables.

"I swear, Jack, if being a private investigator ever gets old, you could be a cook." Dixie laughed. "With one specialty, of course."

"Actually…" Jack paused as he took another swallow of wine. "I've been thinking seriously about a different way of making a living."

Dixie stayed quiet, hoping it would encourage him to share.

"Emma and I were planning to make the lodge a viable way to give us both a new start."

Trying to keep from choking, Dixie chewed as though the morsel were manna from heaven. A fresh start...for he and Emma. She'd lost her heart to a man who was unavailable.

It wasn't fair, it wasn't right, but Dixie would not seduce a man away from another if that was where his heart lay.

"Emma needs a change." Jack's expression softened. "She certainly deserves it."

Dixie choked. And good. Feeling tears well in her eyes, she thumped her chest to dislodge the piece of potato.

Jack stood. "Dixie, are you choking?"

Evidently her expression answered his question, because instantly Jack was behind her, yanking her to her feet, wrapping his arms around her front and thrusting upward with his clenched fists.

"Humph." Dixie gasped as the block flew from her throat and she could breathe again. Had she actually just spit out food in front of the man she was hot for?

"Are you okay?" Jack supported her still.

Dixie took in the pallor beneath his tan. "All in the line of duty, eh?" Her voice emerging husky and soft. "Thank you."

"Jeez, woman. You gave me a heart attack." Jack circled around to his place on the quilt.

Dixie took a drink of wine and tried to recall the statement that had sent her into a choking fit.

"Jack," Dixie started. "...about Emma."

"My aunt." Jack stared at her. "What about her?"

Dixie couldn't answer. Laughter welled up. Then bubbled forth.

"Dixie, are you choking again?" Jack started to stand.

Waving him off before he could bruise her mid-section again, Dixie dabbed at her eyes and tried to stop the giggles as he relaxed.

"I'm…sorry…it's just that I thought…" She stopped, and took a breath, "I thought Emma was your blond, busty secretary you were involved with."

Jack stared. "What in the world gave you that idea?"

"Well you never actually shared who she was before."

"You don't have a mouth to ask?" Jack was smiling now, understanding the confusion Dixie had felt over his "Emma."

"Well…I…" Dixie sipped more wine knowing that her tingling lips and fingertips were a signal to eat more, drink less. "I didn't feel I had a right to ask about the woman who might be in your life."

Realizing she'd been a lot more open than she'd planned, Dixie concentrated on cutting another bite of steak to avoid Jack's gaze.

"Dixie." Jack waited for her to look up from her plate. "I'm not involved with anyone. You are."

And at that exact moment, Dixie knew she was sunk. With no "other woman," how could she talk her heart out of falling even more for Jack.

For the next two hours, Dixie kept quiet about Guy

not actually being her fiancé, realizing it was the last protection her heart had left. She shared anecdotes about the teens she worked with, as well as Maggie and her mother. Jack lay on his side and listened. Then he opened up when Dixie would venture a question.

By the time the meal was finished and the bottle of wine drained, Dixie was in trouble.

With a capital "T."

Cleaning the plates from the meal together, a comfortable quiet settled over them. Jack became quiet, glancing at Dixie occasionally. And frowning.

Why is he frowning at me?

Checking for pieces of food between her teeth with the tip of her tongue, Dixie enjoyed the lethargy brought on by the good food, excellent wine and stimulating company.

Finally there was no more to put away. Nothing to delay a decision. Dixie stood, feeling awkward near the kitchen door.

Jack put the lid on the cooler and turned to look at her. With sure steps he walked to stand in front of her. With a hand he cupped her cheek, and tilted her face upward until Dixie was forced to meet his gaze.

"Do you know I want you?" Jack's question was softly spoken, but direct.

Dixie shuddered and placed her hand over his against her cheek. "Yes..."

Leaning closer, Jack gave her the space and seconds if she wanted to stop what was inevitable. Dixie stood firm.

When his lips touched hers, the taste was more intoxicating than the wine…and a million times more potent. Deepening the touch, Jack moved closer at the same time she did…echoing a need shared.

Then, it was over.

"Good night, Dixie." Jack placed one more soft kiss on the side of her neck. "Go on up, I'll walk the dogs and see you in the morning."

Leaving her breathless and confused, Jack left the kitchen and walked outside.

Dixie stood dazed. What had just happened? The signals were there…and he'd walked away. Why?

Thoughts of her "engagement" to Guy must have helped Jack decide to stay distant. It's what she'd wanted by telling the white lie. Wasn't it?

So, why did she suddenly wish she'd never made it up?

Dixie woke the next morning to the sound of birds. She stretched both arms above her head in the narrow bed.

Despite the desire for Jack that she'd carried to bed, Dixie had drifted off almost immediately. The combination of wine and warm down comforters cradling her into a deep sleep…though a sleep filled with sensual dreams of Jack.

Dixie wondered at the sense of dread in her heart after waking from such a deep sleep. Why would that be there on such a beautiful day?

Because this was the day.

The coin toss.

The time when she had to make a decision. Actually there was no decision to make. Dixie would not destroy Jack's dream, she couldn't. You didn't do that to someone you loved.

Loved.

Loved?

She loved Jack.

Oh, criminy. How had this sneaked up on her? It was too soon in her life plan. As if fate ever bothered to warn you before it smacked one between the eyes with a two-by-four.

A knock sounded on her door.

"Dixie, are you awake yet?" Estelle's voice sounded on the other side of the door.

What was her mother doing here so early?

The door opened and Estelle entered the room. Smiling, she sat on the edge of Dixie's bed. "Honey, you have fifteen minutes to be downstairs before that lummox of a lawyer tosses that coin without you."

Dixie sat upright. "What time is it?"

"Nearly noon." Estelle looked at her closely. "Jack is waiting downstairs with the man with the quarter, or whatever he has."

"I love Jack."

"I know that, it's why you told him you were engaged to another man." Estelle sat straighter. "Tell me something I don't know."

"How did you know?"

"For heaven's sake, you two are so obvious." She patted Dixie's hand. "The question is what are you going to do about it?"

Mr. Granger waited in the car, a pale-faced underling waiting with him. Jack and Dixie approached as the men stepped out of the car. Dixie had avoided meeting his eyes since she'd flown downstairs after throwing her clothes and a baseball cap on.

So much for glamour.

Mr. Granger offered Jack his hand. "Good morning, glad to see you both still here."

Jack didn't smile. "Can we get on with it?"

Dixie flinched. It was obvious Jack wanted nothing more than to be away from her. Well, it would happen soon enough. First, she had to give him the only gift she could.

Mr. Granger turned to his assistant. "You have the coin?"

The younger man removed a small box from his suit coat pocket. "Right here, sir."

Mr. Granger took the coin from the box. "All right. The rules are simple. When I flip the coin into the air the two of you will call heads or tails. If you should call the same thing, we will do it again."

Dixie looked back at the porch where her mother waited with Vincent. Estelle gave her a thumbs up. Jack's jaw was clenched and he didn't look her way.

Glancing at them both, Mr. Granger flipped the coin into the air. Sunlight turned the rotating edges into diamonds. Then they were blocked out as a hand pulled the coin from the air.

"What in the world? Sir, you cannot do that." Mr. Granger was flushed.

"Yes, sir, I can." Jack tossed the coin into the trees without looking at it. "I won't destroy Dixie's dream. She needs this lodge for the kids. She has it. I forfeit."

Dixie stared at him with her mouth open. He'd stolen her thunder, robbed her of the chance to do that same thing for him. Why had he done it?

"Jack, that's kind of you, but I want you to have the lodge." Dixie could feel her pulse pounding in her ears. Why had he given her the lodge?

"Dixie, I'm trying to be noble here. I know you're engaged, but I love you. I want you to be happy, with or without me. The lodge is your dream for the kids, make it happen." Jack stood with his hands clenched into fists by his sides.

"Oh for the love of Michael." Estelle could stand it no longer, would no one tell these idiots what was going on? "You, Dixie, told me just now that you love this man. You aren't really engaged to Guy, you only made it up to keep some distance from Jack. Hello. Am I the only one who—oh."

She smiled as Jack lifted Dixie from her feet, wrapped her in his arms and kissed her.

Vincent pulled on Estelle's arm. "Let's go for a walk. I hear there's a lovely spring through the trees."

Estelle walked beside her Vinnie. She glanced back. Jack and Dixie were still oblivious to the world and the other two men were climbing back into their car, shaking their heads as if they didn't understand what was happening. Well, they probably didn't.

It looked as though Jack and Dixie would make their dreams come true together with the lodge. Bill would finally see happiness and children in the lodge he'd built and Vinnie held her hand.

All was well.

EPILOGUE

Dixie listened to the sounds of rock music and laughter drifting through the lodge.

Had it really only been seven weeks since the coin toss?

Listening to the four teens that were refinishing the kitchen cabinets while laughing, Dixie set the cloth back in the bucket. The windows could wait.

Out in the yard, Jack was measuring a length of board for the new front porch steps while Bill cut with the electric saw.

Bill was still quiet, but opening more each day while helping to update the lodge for the new retreat center for troubled teens.

"Dixie…"

A soft voice broke into Dixie's quiet time.

"Emma…I'm just resting." Dixie smiled at the other woman, amazed at the zest and energy the older woman possessed.

"It's time." Emma's excitement was tangible.

"Oh, my, gosh…" Dixie jumped out of the rocker and followed Emma to the master bedroom Dixie shared with her new husband, Jack.

In the corner, Sadie lay on her side in a soft bed of old quilts…ready to deliver the pups she and Tigger were expecting.

"It's okay...easy..." Dixie stroked Sadie's head, wanting to help but feeling helpless.

A hand on her shoulder pulled Dixie's attention for a moment...Jack. He smiled down at her and she melted...still.

Emma touched her knee and redirected her attention. With wonderment, Dixie watched the first pup emerge...orange striped and tiny...a miniature replica of Tigger.

Jack crouched next to her and they helped their new family enter the world.

All nine of them.

0205/02

MILLS & BOON®

Live the emotion

Tender romance™

A FAMILY FOR KEEPS by Lucy Gordon *(Heart to Heart)*

Vincenzo saw that Julia had been to hell and back. It was up to
him to show her how wonderful the world could be. Julia never
thought she would laugh again…or kiss a gorgeous man. But she
did – with Vincenzo! Life was perfect – then Vincenzo made a
shocking discovery…

THE BUSINESS ARRANGEMENT by Natasha Oakley

For as long as Amy has known Hugh Balfour, she's loved him.
Her strategy was to avoid him at all costs – but now he needs a
PA…and only Amy will do! But he expects twenty-four-hour
attention – especially now he's looking at his old friend in a *very*
different light!

FIRST PRIZE: MARRIAGE by Jodi Dawson

When Dixie Osborn enters a competition to win a secluded
mountain lodge, she never expects to win! She's thrilled – but
there's a catch… Dixie's ticket was stuck to another – there's a
tie! Now she has to share the lodge with the totally gorgeous Jack
Powers for four days…

THE BLIND-DATE SURPRISE by Barbara Hannay

(Southern Cross)

The loneliness of the Outback is driving Annie McKinnon crazy.
How is a woman supposed to find love when the nearest eligible
man lives miles away? When she meets her dream man over the
Internet, she wants to dash to the city to meet him. But her blind
date has a secret…

On sale 4th March 2005

*Available at most branches of WHSmith, Tesco, ASDA, Martins,
Borders, Eason, Sainsbury's and all good paperback bookshops.*

Visit www.millsandboon.co.uk

EXtra

Favourite, award-winning or bestselling authors. Bigger reads, bonus short stories, new books or much-loved classics. *Always* **fabulous reading!**

Don't miss:

EXTRA passion for your money! (March 2005)
Emma Darcy – Mills & Boon Modern Romance
NEW *Mistress to a Tycoon* and **CLASSIC** *Jack's Baby*

EXTRA special for your money! (April 2005)
Sherryl Woods – Silhouette Special Edition –
Destiny Unleashed. This **BIG** book is about a woman
who is finally free to choose her own path…love,
business or a little sweet revenge?

EXTRA tender for your money! (April 2005)
Betty Neels & Liz Fielding – Mills & Boon
Tender Romance – **CLASSIC** *The Doubtful Marriage*
and **BONUS**, *Secret Wedding*
Two very popular writers write two very different,
emotional stories on the always-bestselling wedding theme.

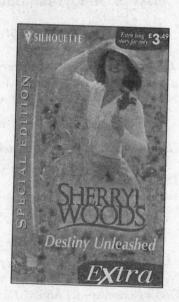

MILLS & BOON

**Volume 10
on sale from
2nd April
2005**

Lynne
Graham

International Playboys

*Bond of
Hatred*

FREE!
4 Books
and a surprise gift!

We would like to take this opportunity to thank you for reading this Mills & Boon® book by offering you the chance to take FOUR more specially selected titles from the Tender Romance™ series absolutely FREE! We're also making this offer to introduce you to the benefits of the Reader Service™—

- ★ **FREE home delivery**
- ★ **FREE gifts and competitions**
- ★ **FREE monthly Newsletter**
- ★ **Exclusive Reader Service offers**
- ★ **Books available before they're in the shops**

Accepting these FREE books and gift places you under no obligation to buy, you may cancel at any time, even after receiving your free shipment. Simply complete your details below and return the entire page to the address below. You don't even need a stamp!

YES! Please send me 4 free Tender Romance books and a surprise gift. I understand that unless you hear from me, I will receive 6 superb new titles every month for just £2.75 each, postage and packing free. I am under no obligation to purchase any books and may cancel my subscription at any time. The free books and gift will be mine to keep in any case.

N5ZEF

Ms/Mrs/Miss/Mr ....Initials...........................

BLOCK CAPITALS PLEASE

Surname ....

Address..

....

....Postcode ....

Send this whole page to:
UK: FREEPOST CN8I, Croydon, CR9 3WZ

Offer valid in UK only and is not available to current Reader service subscribers to this series. Overseas and Eire please write for details. We reserve the right to refuse an application and applicants must be aged 18 years or over. Only one application per household. Terms and prices subject to change without notice. Offer expires 30th June 2005. As a result of this application, you may receive offers from Harlequin Mills & Boon and other carefully selected companies. If you would prefer not to share in this opportunity please write to The Data Manager, PO Box 676, Richmond, TW9 1WU.

Mills & Boon® is a registered trademark owned by Harlequin Mills & Boon Limited.
Tender Romance™ is being used as a trademark. The Reader Service™ is being used as a trademark.